Cheaper To Keep Her 5

Also by Kiki Swinson

Playing Dirty
Notorious
Wifey
I'm Still Wifey
Life After Wifey
Still Wifey Material
A Sticky Situation
The Candy Shop
Wife Extraordinaire
Wife Extraordinaire Returns
Cheaper to Keep Her
Cheaper to Keep Her 2
Cheaper to Keep Her 3
Cheaper to Keep Her 4
The Score
The Mark

Anthologies

Sleeping with the Enemy (with Wahida Clark)
Heist (with De'nesha Diamond)
Heist 2 (with De'nesha Diamond)
Lifestyles of the Rich and Shameless (with Noire)
A Gangster and a Gentleman (with De'nesha Diamond)
Most Wanted (with Nikki Turner)
Still Candy Shopping (with Amaleka McCall)
Fistful of Benjamins (with De'nesha Diamond)
Schemes (with Saundra)

Published by Kensington Publishing Corp.

Kiki
Swinson

Dafina
BOOKS

Kensington Publishing Corp.
www.kensingtonbooks.com

DAFINA BOOKS are published by

Kensington Publishing Corp.
119 West 40th Street
New York, NY 10018

All Kensington Titles, Imprints, and Distributed Lines are available at special quantity discounts for bulk purchases for sales promotions, premiums, fund-raising, and educational or institutional use. Special book excerpts or customized printings can also be created to fit specific needs. For details, write or phone the office of the Kensington special sales manager: Kensington Publishing Corp., 119 West 40th Street, New York, NY 10018, attn: Special Sales Department, Phone: 1-800-221-2647.

Dafina and the Dafina logo Reg. U.S. Pat. & TM Off.

ISBN-13: 978-1-4967-0076-6
ISBN-10: 1-4967-0076-7
First Kensington Mass Market Edition: March 2017

10 9 8 7 6 5 4 3 2 1

Printed in the United States of America

Prologue

I had just escaped from a safe house that was heavily guarded by FBI agents and ended up in a taxicab with a fucking serial killer. Fear stricken, I panicked. I grabbed the door handle and started flicking it back and forth while I forced my weight on the door, but it wouldn't budge. "Let me out," I screamed.

The only response I got from the taxi driver was a mechanical laugh while he stared at me in his rearview mirror. I wanted so desperately to attack the man, but the glass that separated the front seat and the back seat prevented me from doing so. So I did the next best thing. I turned my body around and started kicking the back door windows as hard as I could, but the glass wouldn't break no matter the amount of force or weight I inflicted on it.

"Let me out of here, you fucking weirdo!" I screamed at the top of my voice. I was quickly losing my freaking mind. It felt like my head was spinning in circles while my stomach was forming knots in its pit. Then, before I knew it, everything around me started moving in slow motion. "Let . . . me . . . go . . . you . . . sick . . . mother . . . fucker!" I spat. My body quickly went into hysterical mode. After everything I've been through this past year with my ex–best friend, Duke Carrington, and Bishop, I couldn't let this man kill me like he did those other women. I was a trooper. I was known to get myself out of anything, so I couldn't let this maniac take control of me.

"Let me the fuck out of here!" I screamed once more as I kicked at the back windows and doors. Unfortunately, my words fell on deaf ears. He completely ignored me and continued to drive where he was planning to take me. Through the tears and the screaming, I tried to concentrate on the direction he was driving and hoped that when he eventually stopped the cab, I'd have a chance to escape. While I tried to remember the route he was taking, I immediately thought back to the first time my life had been threatened. It was by a man I loved: Duke Carrington. He was the reason why I was on the run for my life. He started this whole journey of mine.

"Bitch! You better open this fucking door!"

When I'd heard his voice, the banging and then the kicking on the door, my heart had sank into the pit of my stomach. A hot flash came over my body at the sound of his deep, baritone voice. I could tell he was more than livid. I'd immediately started rushing through the luxury high-rise condominium I had been living in for the past six months. Duke owned it. It was time to put my Plan B into motion. Quick, fast, and in a hurry.

"Damn, damn, shit!" I'd cursed as I gathered shit up. I didn't know how I had let myself get caught slipping. I'd planned to be the fuck out of Dodge before Duke could get wind of my bad deeds. I had definitely not planned my escape correctly.

"Open the fucking door!" he screamed again.

I was shaking all over. From the sound of his voice I could tell he wasn't fucking around.

"Shit!" I'd whispered as I slung my bag of money over my shoulder and thought about my escape. I whirled around aimlessly but soon realized that my Plan B didn't include Duke being at the front door of his fifth-floor condo. There was nowhere for me to go. There was only one way in and one way out, and I damn sure wasn't jumping off the balcony. If it was the second floor, maybe I would've taken a chance, but I wasn't trying to die.

I spun around and around repeatedly, trying

to get my thoughts together before the hinges gave in to his brute power. Hiding the money I had stolen was paramount. My mind kept beating that thought in my head. I'd raced into the master bedroom and rushed into the walk-in closet. I began frantically snatching clothes off the hangers. I needed to use them to hide my bag of cash.

Wham!

"Oh, my God!" I'd blurted out when I'd heard the front door slam open with a clang. I threw the bag onto the floor and covered it with piles of designer clothes—things Duke and I had shopped for together when shit was good between us.

"Bitch, you thought I was playing with you?" Duke's powerful voice had roared. "Didn't I tell you you had to get the fuck out of my crib?"

He was up on me within seconds. I'd stood defenseless as he advanced on me so fast, I didn't even have time to react. I threw my hands up, trying to shield myself from what I expected to come when he reached out for me. But I was too late. He'd grabbed me around my neck so hard and tight, I could swear little pieces of my esophagus had crumbled.

"Duke, wait!" I'd said in a raspy voice as he squeezed my neck harder. I'd started scratching at his big hands, trying to free myself so I could breathe.

"What, bitch? I told you if you ever fucked with me, you wouldn't like it!" he snarled. Tears immediately rushed down my face as I fought for air. "Ain't no use in crying now. You should've thought 'bout that shit a long time ago."

Duke finally released me with a shove. I went stumbling back and fell on my ass so hard, it started throbbing. I tried to scramble up off the floor, but before I could get my bearings I felt his hands on me again. His strong hand was winding into my long hair.

"Ouch!" I'd wailed, bending my head to try to relieve some of the pressure he was putting on my head.

Duke yanked me up by my hair. Sharp, stabbing pains shot through my scalp.

"Owww!" I'd cried out as he wrung me around. I tried to put my small hands on top of his huge, animal hands, but it was no use. Hands I had once loved I now despised and wished would just fall off.

"You thought it was all good, right! You a fucking trifling-ass bitch, and I want you the fuck out of here!" Duke gritted. Then he'd lifted his free hand and slapped me across my face with all his might.

"Pl-pl-pl-please!" I'd begged him for mercy. But Duke hit me again.

I was crying hysterically. Partly from the pain of his abuse. I would have never thought our relationship would come to this. It had been a long road, and all I wanted to do was teach him a lesson when I did the shit I did. I never thought he would treat me like that after the way I loved him. But the abuse had continued until he was killed.

Now, once again, I was in harm's way. I couldn't let this cab driver do me in. No way. I knew I was going to have to fight him to the death.

Chapter 1

Witness Protection

"**W**hich fucking way did she run?" I yelled. My voice boomed while my heart raced uncontrollably as I searched every inch of the backyard of the safe house.

"She climbed over the fence and ran north up the alley toward Cleveland Street," Agent Rome answered as he snapped to, having been caught lounging while their charge was on the run.

"How the hell did she get out of here? Was the alarm not working?" I continued to question Agent Rome while I made a dash toward the fence. Agent Rome followed my lead.

"I'm gonna take Wingate and see if I can cut her off there." I heard Agent Zachary's voice as she joined the chase.

"Keep your radio on," I yelled back at her.

"I will," she quickly replied.

Agent Rome and I sprinted up the alleyway that led to Cleveland Street and made a quick right turn. I scanned the entire block with hopes of spotting Lynise's movements. But it was to no avail; she was nowhere in sight. I immediately panicked and spun around in a complete circle to catch my breath. "Where the fuck could she have gone?" I growled as I set my sights on Agent Rome. I tried to slow my heart rate down as I controlled my breathing, but it didn't work. It felt like I was completely winded.

He stood there panting like he was out of breath too. "Maybe she's heading toward the highway, hoping to get a ride to Norfolk," Agent Rome replied.

"That may be true, but for now we're gonna search this area thoroughly. My gut tells me that she's somewhere close by. So, go back to the house and round up all the agents except for Humphreys and tell them to get in their cars and comb through every block within five miles of the house."

"Will do," Agent Rome said, and then scrambled back to the safe house.

I continued down Cleveland Street. The streets were pitch black, except for the dim streetlight at the corner of Cleveland and Monroe Streets. As I approached the streetlight, I saw a silhouette of a woman. My gun was already drawn. "Put your hands up and identify yourself," I demanded.

The moving object stopped. "Foster, don't shoot! It's me, Zachary," she yelled.

"Show your face," I instructed her.

"Okay. I'm coming in slowly," she replied.

I kept my pistol aimed, cocked, and ready while I waited for Agent Zachary to reveal herself. After I confirmed her identity, I let out a long sigh and lowered my weapon. "Did you clear the area east of the safe house?" I asked her.

"Yes, I did."

"And you didn't see her anywhere?"

"Nope. But I ran into a few junkies who said that they haven't seen anyone running around here fitting her description."

"That's bullshit. They saw her," I growled.

Agent Zachary gave me this "I told you so" look. "You just don't want to take the blame, huh?"

"What blame?" I replied. I knew where Zachary was going with this, so I tried to play the dumb role.

"Foster, cut it out. You know you screwed up with this entire operation. Your little Miss Witness fucked you, played you for a fool, and now she's gone on her merry way."

"Zachary, you have absolutely no idea what you are talking about. Lynise is only a witness that I have been assigned to protect. That's it. And when we get her back in our custody, that's how things will resume. So let's not have this conversation again. Now, are we clear on that?"

"Why are you getting so defensive?"

"Zachary, you know I am not being defensive. I just want us to have a mutual understanding," I replied.

"Oh, we have a mutual understanding, but it seems like every time your little girlfriend throws a fit, you always make special provisions for her."

"Zachary, I will not continue to have this conversation with you. Right now we need to use every resource we have to find our witness before the wrong people do."

"Yes, sir," she said sarcastically, and then she gave me a grimace. She wasn't feeling me, or Lynise for that matter. She hated Lynise. She was jealous of her too. And if it were up to her, she'd call this whole search off and go to her next assignment.

After Zachary said what she had to say, I ignored her. I learned a long time ago how to deal with Agent Zachary. She was very territorial. She'd always act out when another woman infringed on her space during a work detail. So every once in a while I'll give her the floor for a few minutes so she can gripe and address certain things that are bothering her. But after that, the issue will be over and done with. Today was no different.

Once I checked Agent Zachary about her feelings concerning Lynise, I put that matter to rest. I looked down at my wristwatch and noticed that I had wasted six damn minutes listening to Zachary fill my head up with a bunch of bullshit about Lynise. I knew every minute from this moment forward was very significant. "Let's go. We've got more ground to cover, so stay on guard," I instructed her.

Agent Zachary and I canvassed every inch of Cleveland Street and the five blocks surrounding it. "Does anyone have a visual?" I spoke into my radio.

"It's clear over here," Agent Rome replied.

"What's your position?" I asked him.

"Washington Street and Pinehurst," he responded.

"Agent Mann, what's your position?" I continued to probe everyone's location.

"I'm in the car circling the entire neighborhood," he replied.

"Well, Mann, stay on patrol until I say otherwise. Rome, I want you to meet me back at the house. It's time to go to Plan B."

"What about Zachary? You do know she's out here too," Rome questioned me.

"Zachary is with me. And we're headed back to the house now."

"Roger that," Rome spoke back through the radio, and then all communication went dead.

Going into search mode!

Chapter 2

My Worst Fucking Nightmare

I knew Agent Sean and the rest of those fake-cop-ass FBI agents were pounding the streets looking for me. But I was in a fucking cab with the serial killer who's been raping and killing women these past couple of months, now trapped in the backseat trying to break through one of these windows. My eyes were very glassy, but I was still able to see which direction we were going.

And after we crossed over the bridge and traveled through the Hampton Bridge Tunnel, I noticed that he took the first exit, which was the Willoughby Spit exit.

In no time, the cab driver had pulled over to the side of the road. I looked around and noticed that the street we were on was deserted.

There was only one streetlight lit on the entire fucking block. The shit looked spooky. And to know that I was with a fucking murderer only made things worse. This guy was a straggly-looking, middle-aged black guy who had to be in his late forties. His facial hair and the hair on his head looked rough and unmanaged. From the backseat, this man looked like he was every bit of 160 pounds, if not more. I could also tell that he didn't have much height to him. After sizing him up I psyched myself into believing that I could take him down.

"Let me out of this fucking car!" I continued to scream while kicking on both the window and the door.

"Bitch, if you break that window I'm going to kill you!" his voice boomed.

"Fuck you! You better let me out of this motherfucking car now!" I screamed as loud as I could. I had to let this bastard know that I wasn't afraid of him.

While I made it blatantly obvious that I wasn't going down without a fight, he in turn showed me that he was ready to go toe-to-toe with me. Out of nowhere this fucking maniac produced a Taser. I saw a spark, then two wires with hooks at the end of them followed. Before I even realized it, fifty thousand volts of electricity hit my body. I tried to fight it, but the movement in my body started slipping away from me. And then it stopped.

Had death finally claimed my life?

Chapter 3

The Manhunt

Once we realized that Lynise wasn't in the immediate area, all of the agents met me back at the safe house. I ordered everyone in the house to gather in the downstairs meeting room. "As we all know, our witness has escaped. What we don't know is her whereabouts. With that said, we're gonna have to gear up and start a full-blown manhunt until she is back in our custody."

"Have you contacted anyone back at headquarters?" Agent Rome asked.

"No, I haven't," I replied.

"Well, don't you think you should?" Rome's questions continued.

"As the senior officer at this safe house, I am in charge of everyone here, so that gives me the discretion to make those types of calls. So, to answer your question, no, I don't think I should call headquarters. I will handle this matter on my own."

"What if we don't find her?" Agent Zachary asked.

"Let's be a little more optimistic, Zachary."

"Foster, she's right. What if we don't find her?" Agent Mann chimed in.

I was starting to get a little aggravated by all of my agents' questions. They noticed it too. "Listen carefully, guys, because I am only going to say this once. Our federal witness has fled on foot, so we're gonna have to gather up all of our resources so that we can find her and bring her back into our custody. Now, if for some unfortunate reason we can't find her, then we will call headquarters. In the meantime, keep your eyes and ears open and make sure everyone's back is covered. We can't have another casualty like we just had when we were escorting our witness back from the police precinct. We have to be in control of everything around us. We cannot afford to ever have that done to us again. Understood?"

"Yes, sir," everyone said in unison.

"Does anyone have any other questions before we leave here?"

"Do you plan to leave an agent here just in case she comes back?" Agent Zachary asked.

"I'm glad you asked, because you were the person I had in mind."

"Me?!" Agent Zachary replied. I could tell by her voice that she was surprised by my suggestion.

"Yes, you."

"But what if she doesn't come back?" Agent Zachary tried to reason. She wasn't at all happy with me.

Whether she knew it or not, it wouldn't be a good look to have her with me anyway. She was indeed a good agent, but she made a lot of her decisions based on emotions. And right now the last thing I needed were emotions. I needed to find my witness, and I refused to let Agent Zachary blow our cover.

Before I could assign additional work details, Agent Rome chuckled and mumbled, "With that large bounty on her head we oughta just let her go. I mean, she'll probably be dead within twenty-four hours anyway."

"Would you mind repeating that, agent?" I spoke up. His words were jumbled, so I didn't hear what Agent Rome said.

"Listen, boss, all I'm saying is, why don't we leave her be? We got popped pretty bad transporting her from that interrogation she had with those local cops the other day. I mean, come on, why risk one of our own? She left here because she didn't want to be here," Rome explained.

"No, Rome, she left because someone screwed up. And for the life of me I'm trying to figure who that was."

"What are you saying?" Agent Zachary blurted out. She seemed curious as to where I was going with this.

"I'm saying that someone in here either dropped the ball or let her go freely and tried to make it look like she escaped on her own," I explained. I scanned every agent's face with every word I uttered.

"So, you're trying to say someone here let her go?" Agent Rome responded defensively.

"Yes, I am. But if you have another explanation, then I'm all ears," I replied with certainty.

"No disrespect, but I think you're out of your damn mind. What agent on this work detail would jeopardize their career over letting a witness go? That's insane."

"Well, if you think I'm insane, then tell me why you were the only one outside when she escaped? And how is it that she was able to get out of the house without the alarm going off?" I asked Rome. I needed some fucking answers, and I needed them now.

"I can't tell you how she got out of the house without the alarm going off. But I do know that you don't give her enough credit," Agent Rome started off. "She's not a walking target for nothing. Even the local homicide detectives want a piece of her ass. They knew she was lying to them when they interrogated her. And if you continue to act like she's a fucking angel instead of the criminal that she is, then we're going at this thing wrong."

I chuckled at Agent Rome's remark. "How do you suggest we should go at it?" I asked. I was very curious to hear what else this idiot had to say. Something wasn't quite right with Agent Rome, and I intended to find out what it was.

"I think we should count our losses and head back up north," Rome added.

"I agree," Agent Zachary said.

"I don't care who agrees with who around here. The fact still remains that she was placed in our custody. She is the only person alive who can help us put Bishop away for life. Does it even bother you that he murdered our commander, Joyce? Knowing that he took her life should be more of a reason for you to want to go out there and find our witness. We could use Lynise in so many ways."

"Yeah, he's right, you guys. We gotta get her back," Agent Humphreys agreed.

"Where do you want us to start looking?" Agent Mann chimed in.

"She's from Norfolk, so I think that's where we need to set our sights," I suggested as I walked over to the closet near the kitchen entryway. The closet contained a briefcase with most of Lynise's personal information stored inside. After I grabbed the contents from the briefcase, I xeroxed the last three addresses where she resided and made copies of addresses of people she knew. We could not leave a stone unturned. And once we were equipped with the information we needed, I assigned work details and we carried on with our mission.

"Can I talk to you alone before you leave?" Agent Zachary asked me.

"Sure," I told her. I instructed Agent Humphreys to wait for me in the car and then I followed Zachary to the kitchen. "What's up?" I asked her.

"I just wanted to say I'm sorry for taking Agent Rome's side."

"You don't have to apologize to me for that. You're entitled to your opinion. So, I'm good."

"You're not mad, are you?"

"Look, Zachary, are we finished here?" I spat. I was becoming annoyed by all of her questions. Time was ticking away rapidly, and I needed to get out of there.

Thankfully she got the hint and told me she was done talking. After I got into the car, I looked back at the safe house and saw Zachary looking through the mini blinds of the living-room window. I knew she was upset with me, but with her thick skin she'd get over it.

Women were so fucking emotional!

Chapter 4

Where Am I?

My entire body ached when I regained consciousness. And when I realized where I was, I wanted to yell for help, but I couldn't. A salty-tasting cloth that looked like it was torn from an old sheet was tied around my mouth and hung down to my chest. Even the smell of it became unbearable. But what really shattered my heart was when I saw the wretched and sordid conditions my kidnapper put me in. I was strapped down in an old-ass wheelchair placed directly beside a filthy sofa chair. A couple of the springs from the sofa stuck out through the cushions. It was a sight for sore eyes. The carpet was severely worn out. The walls were covered in old wooden paneling. There was also a huge clutter of relatives' pictures nailed to the walls. The lamp shades had old-school fringes hanging from them.

The house wasn't that big. I could see the kitchen from where I was sitting. The refrigerator was an old green color. The kitchen table set was even outdated. The stove was on its last leg too. Every piece of furniture and ceiling fixture in this place looked like it had been purchased back when Kennedy was president. Picture a house from a fucking horror movie and, well, that is what this place reminded me of.

"Honey, she's awake," I heard an older lady say with a heavy southern drawl. Her voice came from the entryway of the TV room, so I turned to see who this voice belonged to. To my surprise, the elderly woman was white. Now, if my memory serves me correctly, the cab driver who dragged me to this horror scene was black. So why is this five-foot-one frail old lady here? She can't be down with this kidnapping shit. I mean, for God's sakes, she looked like she couldn't harm a fly.

Seconds later, I heard footsteps scurrying across the floor behind me, and then the cab driver appeared in front of my eyes. He smiled at me as he began to pull my hair back away from my face. The old white lady stood next to him. She looked like she was taking inventory or something. "Isn't she beautiful, Mama?" he asked.

"Yeah, she looks better than those last two you brought here. What's her name?" she replied.

"Pam."

"Stop fucking touching me!" I belted out. My words were jumbled up because of the gag tied around my mouth.

"Sounds like she's trying to say something," I heard her say.

"She's probably saying she loves me, Mama," the guy commented as he continued to touch my hair. He was giddy, to say the least.

"Are you fucking people crazy? I didn't say I loved him," I screamed. But once again, these psycho-ass people weren't hearing my words. I mean, did he really believe that I uttered the word *love*? Was he out of his fucking mind? And why the hell is she standing here with this crazy-ass man like everything is peachy? And what does she mean the last two girls? Am I not getting out of this motherfucking place alive?

"Where did you get her from?"

"I picked her up in Newport News."

"Well, she's probably hungry," the old lady said.

"Yeah, you're right, Mama. Her face does look like she's famished," the fucking cab driver replied.

"I don't want none of y'alls fucking food! I want y'all to let me go!" I screamed once more. This time tears began to fall. I was becoming so overwhelmed. I was literally about to have a nervous breakdown.

"Oh, Mama, why do you think she's crying?"

the guy asked. He looked somewhat concerned. Seeing me cry made it seem as if he was having second thoughts about kidnapping me.

"I don't know, child. Maybe she misses her mama."

"Are you missing your mama?" the guy asked.

I nodded my head, letting him know that that wasn't it.

"Then what is it?" he pressed the issue.

"I want you to let me go!" I screamed, even though I knew they wouldn't understand me.

Thankfully he loosened the gag from my mouth. It hung around the chin area of my face. I felt some kind of relief. "Listen to me. I am not hungry. And I don't miss my mama. I want to go home," I pleaded with them while I continued to cry.

"But why do you want to go home?" he asked.

"Because I miss my family, and they're gonna wanna know where I'm at," I lied.

"But what about me? What about my feelings?" he questioned me.

"I'm not trying to hurt your feelings. I mean, we can still see each other." I continued to conjure up lies.

"No. I don't believe you. You're gonna leave me just like all the others," he snapped. His whole demeanor changed. He went from acting like a nice guy to an abusive weirdo in the blink of an eye.

"I promise I won't leave you," I tried to convince him.

"No. Shut up! You're a liar just like all of those other girls!" he screamed, and then he abruptly yanked on the gag and forced it back around my mouth.

After he made the gag tighter he stormed off into another part of the house. His mother continued to stand there before me. "You think you're too good for my son, don't cha?" She gritted her teeth.

I shook my head.

"Well, you're acting like it, missy. But let me tell you something. My boy is special. He's a good boy. And I won't let anybody else hurt him. You understand me?" she yelled, and then she smacked me across my face as hard as she could. I swear I saw stars. My vision became blurry as I watched her leave the room. When I was able to hone back in on my surroundings, I was alone once again.

I could not believe how I got myself into yet another deadly situation. First, I was running from Duke Carrington. But after I had him ambushed and done away with, the Carter brothers put a bounty on my head. And once I turned on Bishop, he got in on the action to get rid of me too. Now I'm here at these psychotic-ass people's house. How bad can my life get? Do I have a death wish? Or was it karma? Whatever it was, I had to get a handle on it before I ended up like Diamond and Bishop's sister. I could hear Diamond's voice then, pleading for her life as if it just happened yesterday. I could also see her face clear as day immediately after Bishop and I walked into her apartment. He and I had already discussed the fact that Diamond was going to be murdered before we left her apartment. I remembered throwing my right hand and it connected squarely with her nose. In my mind, I had suddenly become Laila Ali. I was throwing combinations—lefts and rights, rights and lefts. I was hitting her ass on top of her head, in her face, on her body. I was in kill mode, and Diamond's grimy ass would have died by my hands if Bishop's homeboy Torch hadn't lifted me up by my armpits and pulled me off that bitch.

I also remembered that after I walked away from Diamond, Bishop had his hand around her throat, lifting her up. He threw her ass hard in a recliner near the television, opposite the wall where the couch was. It was a new recliner since I lived there.

I got a look at her face, and strange as it was, I felt good. Her face was completely swollen from the beating I had given her monkey ass. Both of her eyes were completely shut. Her face was beet red. But that didn't stop Bishop from asking her a barrage of questions. *Did you set up Neeko to get killed? Who killed him? What part did you play in it? Where was Duke hiding out? Were Duke and Chrissy hiding out together?* I didn't remember every word she said, but I knew that it was good enough for Bishop, because after she finished talking he gave Torch the head nod and seconds later Torch snapped Diamond's neck. She died on the spot. So, was I about to meet the same fate as Diamond did? Whatever was about to happen, I knew I had to brace myself for it.

According to the clock on the wall in the TV room, the serial killer and his crazy-ass mama left me in the room for almost two hours. It had been a total of nine hours since I escaped the safe house. I was starving and I had to pee badly. I battled with the decision about whether or not I should tell those crazy-ass people that I had to use the bathroom. My gut feelings told me that that wouldn't be a good idea. The way these people were bugging out, they'd want to accompany me in the bathroom while I took a piss. The idea of having either one of them watch me pee gave me an eerie feeling. I knew then that I needed to try to hold my urine as long as possible.

Twenty more minutes passed before I heard movements from those fucking weirdos. The serial killer appeared first. He smiled at me like he was happy to see me. Did he just not leave out of here like he wanted to kill me? I wasn't a doctor, but something told me that this crazy-ass nigga was bipolar.

"Hi there, beautiful. I missed you," he said as he approached me.

I wanted to vomit in my mouth after he told me he missed me. Nigga, you were in the next room. And you just saw me not even two hours ago. Get your act together and let me go.

"Are you hungry? Can I get you anything?" he asked me after taking the gag from my mouth.

"I just want to go home." I began to cry, tears falling quickly.

"What are you talking about? You're already home," he replied.

"No, I am not. This is not my home. Please let me go." I cried harder.

"I'm sorry, but I can't do that. You are my soul mate. We're going to be together forever."

"No, we are not. You don't even know me."

"Yes, I do. And you are the one for me."

"Stop saying that. I am not the one for you. I am not your soul mate. So just get that through your head."

Saying nothing about my comments, he grabbed me by my throat and began to choke me. He was squeezing the breath out of me and I was growing weaker and weaker. "So you are not my soul mate, huh?"

I tried to answer him, but I couldn't get a word out. I had to figure out how I was going to get this man to stop choking the life out of me.

"I'm sorry. Yes we are soul mates," I uttered.

My words were barely audible. But thank God he heard me.

At that moment, he loosened his grip from around my neck. I felt kind of relieved, even though the pain was excruciating. I coughed for about three consecutive minutes.

"Aaaahhhh, are you okay?" he asked me while he massaged my neck. This guy was fucking nuts.

I tried to speak between coughs, but I couldn't. So I nodded my head.

What I really wanted to do was tell this guy to get his fucking hands away from me. I mean, how can you try to kill me with your bare hands one minute and then try to console me the next minute? This guy was definitely off his rocker.

"What's going on in here?" his mother blurted out as she entered the TV room.

"Oh, I was just standing here asking my wife-to-be if she was hungry."

"For Christ's sake, Jimmy, it's ten o'clock in the morning. Of course she's hungry," she continued.

"Well, what do we get her?" Jimmy wanted to know.

"Give her some of that oatmeal in there," his mother suggested.

"But what if she doesn't eat it?" Jimmy said.

She slapped him across his shoulder. "Boy, don't question me. Just do what I say," she instructed him.

Jimmy scrambled out of the TV room after his psycho-ass mother demanded that he get me a bowl of oatmeal. "You're gonna love my oatmeal. I've been making it for Jimmy since he was very young," she told me.

"Who cares?!" I said underneath my breath.

"Did you sass me, young lady?" his mother asked me. She leaned over in my face like she wanted to smack me again.

"No, ma'am," I replied, still feeling the throbbing pain around my neck.

"You better not. Because me and my boy will not stand for anyone else disrespecting us. Do you understand?"

"Yes, ma'am."

"Good."

"I need to use the bathroom," I managed to say. I couldn't hold it any longer.

"Jimmy, come on back in here and take this girl to the bathroom," the lady yelled.

"No. Don't call him. I would rather have you take me."

"Oh no. I'm an old lady. I'm not strong enough to push you in that wheelchair."

"I'm not that heavy." I tried to convince her.

"You look heavy to me," she replied. She was adamant about not taking me to the bathroom, which was a load of crap because she smacked the hell out of me earlier. So to stand there and act like she's too weak to push me to the bathroom is pure bullshit!

Jimmy entered the room carrying a bowl of

oatmeal with a spoon in the bowl. "She's gotta use the bathroom?" he asked.

"Yeah. And she tried to get me to take her. But I told her I wasn't pushing her heavy butt. She won't throw my back out."

"Yeah, Mama, I don't want you doing anything." Jimmy sat the bowl of oatmeal down on the coffee table a few feet away from me. Then he took the locks off the wheels and began to push me in the direction of the hallway. The bathroom was only a few feet from the TV room. So as he pushed me down the hall, the wood floor started cracking like it wanted to give way at that moment. I held my breath a few times, hoping that I wouldn't fall through the floor.

After Jimmy stopped the wheelchair in front of the bathroom, he untied my hands and feet. Boy, what a relief that was. "Now I'm gonna let you go in there by yourself, but you better not do anything stupid," he told me.

"I won't," I said as I got up from the chair.

Once inside the bathroom I didn't turn on the light, because it was fully lit by the sun shining through a very small window with bars sealing it from any intruders from the outside. The bathroom itself was filthy. There was no tile left on the floor. It was completely chipped away. There were several rotten boards coming up from the floor, which brought in a major wind draft from underneath the house. The boards were very weak, so I walked around them.

Before I sat down on the toilet I looked at

the seat cover and then I looked down inside the rusty toilet bowl. The sight of it was revolting. It made me sick to my stomach. I couldn't imagine how long this damn thing hadn't been cleaned. "Look now, are you gonna pee or what? 'Cause I ain't got all day," Jimmy said. He stood there with the bathroom door slightly ajar as if he planned to watch my every move.

"Are you going to stand there while I pee?" I got up the nerve to ask him.

Jimmy cracked a smile. "Don't tell me you're scared to pee in front of me."

"No, I am not scared. I just need a little privacy."

"What do you need privacy for? We're not going to hide things from one another. We're going to be together forever," he continued to explain. But I wasn't trying to hear that. I wanted to use the bathroom without being watched, so he needed to get it through his head sooner than later. Before I gave him a rebuttal, I reminded myself that I couldn't be sarcastic. This guy needed to be handled differently. I knew I had to handle him with kid gloves in order to get what I needed. So I took a deep breath and said, "Listen, Jimmy, I know you and I are soul mates. And I know that we're going to be together, but there are some things that women have to have, and one of those things is privacy. All I'm trying to do is use the bathroom and freshen up so I can look good for you while I'm eating breakfast. That's it. So are you going to give me that?" I asked, trying to act like he was in control. Reverse psychology was a very needed tactic at this moment.

After Jimmy thought for a few seconds, he ended up giving me the green light to use the bathroom alone. "I'm gonna let you use the bathroom by yourself, but remember what I said. No funny business."

"Trust me, I won't," I convinced him.

Once the bathroom door was shut, I exhaled. I felt a sense of freedom even though I was locked up in these people's house. All kinds of thoughts rushed through my head. It was hard to think straight. The bottom line was that I needed to figure out a way to get out of this fucking place. And in order to do that, I needed to win his trust.

Winning Jimmy's trust would be easy. But getting his mother's trust was going to be very hard. I could tell that she wasn't feeling me from the start. And when it came to her son, she'd be even more aggressive to shut things down. So I figured that if I got Jimmy to side with me, maybe I'd be able to put a wedge between them and ultimately gain my freedom. It was a game worth playing.

It took me longer than usual to pee. I had to squat over the toilet seat to prevent my ass from touching it, which in turn caused me to pee around the toilet seat and on the floor. What was even worse about this situation was that these people didn't even have toilet paper so I could wipe my ass. To prevent Jimmy from having an excuse to come into the bathroom, I tried to shake as much urine off me as I could, and then I pulled my panties and my pants back up. I didn't bother to flush the toilet, because it didn't look like it worked. I did what most niggas do, shake it off and keep it moving. "I'm done," I said to Jimmy, who was waiting outside the bathroom door.

He opened the door. "Are you ready?" he asked.

"Yes," I replied, and took a seat in the wheelchair.

He wheeled me back into the TV room and fed me the oatmeal after he tied my wrists and ankles back up.

I had to get away from these inbred motherfuckers!

Chapter 5

I Got a Bad Feeling

It was my call to go out and do a full-scale search for Lynise. I could give a dozen different reasons why she needed to be found. That my ass was on the line would be the first one. The second reason was that I had developed feelings for her, and if I was unable to find her before those goons got to her, then I'd be fucked up for life. Figuring out how she got away still bothered me too. I knew Agent Rome wasn't being straight with me. I'd bet money he had something to do with her leaving the safe house. And if that was the case, then it would soon come out.

Agent Humphreys and I drove in one car while Agents Rome and Mann rode in the car behind us. I was glad that Humphreys and I were alone, because I had some questions for him. "You've worked with Rome before, right?"

"Yeah."

"What do you know about him?"

"Well, all I know is that he got transferred to our office a little over a year ago. And Agent Reed paired him up with Agent Mann not too long after that."

"Do you think he's trustworthy?"

"I haven't heard anything bad about him."

"Well I think he had something to do with Lynise getting away."

"What do you think happened?"

"I can't exactly say what happened. But I do know that he had something to do with the alarm system. Lynise didn't know how to disarm it. So there's no doubt in my mind that Rome was behind it. And besides that, how is it that he was the only one who knew Lynise was escaping? Why didn't he let one of us know that he was outside?"

Agent Humphreys thought for a moment and then he said, "It's kind of hard for me to point a finger at Rome, but when I think back to what he said about her running away, he made me a little suspicious."

"Yeah, he's hiding something and I'm going to find out what it is," I assured him.

"I would too. But while you're doing that just tread lightly, because Agent Rome holds a lot of weight within the bureau."

"I don't care what he holds," I snapped. "If he had anything to do with her escaping, then he will get dealt with," I continued. I had to make sure Humphreys knew that Lynise was a high-priority witness. If Rome tampered with our operation in any way, there was going to be a price to pay.

Lynise initially worked as a bartender at a strip club called Magic City, so that was where we began our search. If there was information to get, then that would be a great place to start. Unfortunately, the club wasn't there. We found a big pile of debris where the club used to be. Humphreys and I got out of the vehicle for a closer look. After our assessment, we realized that the place had been burned down.

"Was it burned down?" Agent Rome asked from the driver's seat of his car.

"Yep. That's exactly what happened," I told him.

"Well, where do you want to go next?" he asked me.

"Let's take a ride through a couple of housing projects and see if we can get lucky. Who knows, maybe we can find someone who will give us an idea of where she could be."

"I personally don't think that would be a good idea," Humphreys pointed out. "If you want to ride around those neighborhoods, then that's one thing. But I don't think looking for people to give us information would be a wise thing to do."

"Okay, well, let's just ride around the areas where her profile has listed as places she most frequents."

"Cool," Humphreys agreed.

By the time three o'clock in the morning rolled around, the agents and I decided to head back to the safe house after we scoured the streets of every housing project of Norfolk and Virginia Beach. When we walked through the doors, Agent Zachary greeted us. "Well, did you find her?" she asked me.

"No."

"Where exactly did you guys go?"

"We searched all of the bad neighborhoods in Norfolk and Virginia Beach."

"Did you stop by the strip club where she was a bartender?"

"That place is no longer there."

"What do you mean it's not there?"

"It was burned down."

"Well what about the other strip clubs in that area? Did you stop by any of them?"

"We stopped by a couple of them. But we got no action."

"So what's next? Are you guys going to do another full search tomorrow?"

"Yeah. We're gonna have to do something. And we're gonna have to do it fast."

"Think it would be a good idea if you reach out to some of her family? Because when I looked into her file I noticed that she had a couple of cousins who lived in Norfolk."

"Yes. But I want that to be the last resort."

"Why?"

"Because I don't want to alarm anyone. And I don't want to let the wrong person know that she is somewhere in the area," I replied while I took off my jacket.

"Well, yeah, that makes sense," she said.

"Well, since I'm gonna have a long day tomorrow, I'm gonna go ahead and turn in so I can get some sleep."

"Me too," Humphreys said.

I noticed Agent Rome and Agent Mann followed suit while Agent Zachary stayed in the living room area of the house.

Immediately after I got into bed I realized that my body wouldn't allow me to sleep. I tossed and turned all night thinking about how I was going to handle things going forward. I meant what I said when I made the comment about reaching out to Lynise's family being my last resort. At this very moment, at least a dozen people were looking for Lynise, so if I wanted to get her back into our custody safely, then that meant that I'd have to take all the necessary precautions. My circle of agents was small, and I liked it that way. You can keep drama to a minimum when you work with a small group of people. The only problem I had with my circle was Agent Rome. He just doesn't carry himself as a trustworthy guy, especially with all of the lame-ass excuses he gave me when I questioned him about when he and Lynise were in the backyard alone. Nothing he said added up to me. So I planned to keep a close watch on him and his partner, Mann, just in case I needed to handle things with them a little differently. I can never be too careful, especially after the first security breach involving Lynise and my other agents Morris and Wise when a fucking old beat-up car crashed into the living-room area of an apartment Lynise was staying in.

It became obvious that someone deliberately drove the car into that apartment. But after the agents looked in the driver's seat for the driver, it was empty. Even worse, Agent Wise was run over by that vehicle and killed instantly. So luckily I and five other agents were only one mile away. We were all dressed in military-issued fatigue gear, bulletproof vests inscribed with FBI and the heaviest, most deadly artillery one man could carry in their arms. We were definitely ready for war.

I grabbed Lynise by the arm and escorted her to a black Suburban with tinted windows. A few of her neighbors stood outside and watched as the events surrounding the crash unfolded.

Immediately after four police officers and two of my agents helped the tow truck driver remove the car from the apartment, the coroners were able to remove Agent Wise's body from the debris. It was an ugly sight. I distinctly remembered Lynise telling me that it looked like she was watching an episode of *CSI*. But it only got worse after finding the body of Bishop's sister, Bria, in the trunk of that car, a bullet wound in her head. And from that moment, I knew I had to put Lynise into the Witness Protection Program.

But what was so crazy was that after I decided to put Lynise in Witness Protection, I instructed Agent Pax and Agent Morris to transport her to a safe location, but the plan fell apart after those two agents decided to stop off at a freaking gas station so that one of them could use the bathroom. And just like that, there was another attempt on Lynise's life.

Instead of Lynise losing her life, one of the agents was executed while Lynise sat in the backseat and watched. The sad part about it was that Bishop had recruited and paid one of our office linguists to be a whistle-blower and kill Lynise herself.

According to witnesses and Lynise, Agent Morris got out of the SUV and walked to the men's restroom inside the service station. Meanwhile a Hispanic- and black-featured woman with long hair pulled up in a Volkswagen Passat and parked it next to a gas pump about a few feet away from the SUV that Lynise and the other agent were sitting in. The Hispanic woman removed a McDonald's bag and a drink cup from her car and threw them into the trash can next to her pump.

Then as Agent Morris made his way out of the service station and back to the SUV, the Hispanic woman caught his eye. They say that Agent Morris talked to the woman for a few minutes. Lynise said she thought Agent Morris was flirting with the woman. But after Agent Pax got a good look at the woman and saw that Agent Morris was talking to Chrissy, the department's linguist specialist, that name triggered something in Lynise's mind.

Lynise told me that before she could figure out where she remembered hearing that name, Agent Morris and Chrissy walked up to the driver's side. After Agent Pax rolled down his window, Chrissy opened her mouth and spoke with a squeaky voice. And that's when it hit Lynise that Chrissy was the exact same woman she talked to on Bishop's cell phone.

Lynise also told me that Chrissy asked the agents where they were taking her, and before either of the agents could answer, Lynise said that she interjected and told them not to tell her because she was working for Bishop. At that very moment, Lynise said that Chrissy pulled out a gun and executed both agents by shooting them in their heads. Witnesses said that Agent Morris's and Agent Pax's brains were splattered all over the front seat and the windshield. Within seconds, Chrissy then tried to murder Lynise.

After three failed attempts to open both back doors, Lynise said that Chrissy tried to shoot the windows out, but she couldn't get them to budge. When Chrissy finally figured out that they were bulletproof, she stuck her gun inside the driver's side window and aimed it at Lynise. Chrissy pulled the trigger, and Lynise ducked behind the seat, but that didn't prevent Lynise from getting hit. The bullet went right through her left shoulder.

Thankfully Chrissy had almost emptied the clip on both agents and the windows. When she tried to kill Lynise, she had only one bullet left, so she fled the scene in that Volkswagen Passat. I don't think I would've been able to live with myself if Lynise had gotten killed by one of our own, which is why I've got to find her. When I took this case I vowed to protect her, and that's what I intend to do.

Chapter 6

These Motherfuckers
Are Crazy

After two days passed in the hellhole with those fucking fruitcakes, I figured out Jimmy's schedule. He would drive his cab at night, and during the day he either slept or worried me the fuck to death. There was not a minute that went by that he didn't express how much his sick ass loves me. On top of that, he brought his mother and me each a dozen red roses when he walked in the house this morning. "Got you and my mama some beautiful roses." He smiled.

His mother smiled too. But I wasn't in the mood to smile. I was tied down to a fucking wheelchair twenty-four hours a day, wearing the same clothes, and I hadn't washed my ass or my face or even brushed my teeth. So I say fuck the roses and give me a one-way ticket out of this joint. I'll be happy once that happens.

Jimmy handed his mother her dozen roses first. After she took them she admired how nice they were and then she thanked him. Instead of placing the roses in my hands, Jimmy set them on my lap, since my hands were tied. "Do you like 'em?" he asked me.

"Yes. They're really pretty," I lied. I could not have cared less about the fucking roses.

"I just got them from this guy down there by the pier."

"I hope you didn't spend a fortune on them," his mother said.

"Oh no. I got a great deal for 'em."

"Put mine in some water," his mother instructed him.

Jimmy took them from her hands. "Want me to put yours in some water too?" he asked as he turned to me.

"Yeah. That's fine."

Jimmy took both my roses and his mother's to the kitchen and stuck them into two vases half filled with water. He brought them back to the TV room and sat them down on the coffee table so that we could see them.

I watched him through my peripheral vision as he smiled at the roses. He admired them like they were huge achievements.

"You did good, son," his mother commented.

"Thank you, Mama. Thank you," he responded.

Jimmy stared at the roses for at least another sixty seconds. When he finally looked away, it was because his mother was excusing herself from the room. "Well, I guess I can go in my room now that you're home," she said as she stood up from the run-down couch.

Jimmy stood up. "Mama, why are you leaving so fast?"

"Because I am tired. I've been sitting in this chair all night long watching this girl for you. So now it's time for me to go and lie down in my own bed."

"Do you need any help?" Jimmy seemed concerned.

"No. I'm fine," she said, and slapped him on his arm like he was irritating her.

"Do you want me to bring some hot tea to your room?"

"No. I've drank enough tea this morning for ten people."

"Okay. Well, let me know if you need me," he told her.

After his mother waddled down the hallway to her room I heard her close her bedroom door. It was like music to my ears. I figured this would be a perfect time to start working on Jimmy. He needed to be broken down slowly. I knew I was dealing with a whack job, so if I screwed up I could forget leaving this place alive. Jimmy turned around and looked at me. "I guess it's just me and you now."

I gave him a fake-ass smile.

"Did Mama feed you breakfast?"

"No. I told her I wanted to wait for you to cook my breakfast," I replied seductively. I had to turn the charm on very thick.

This made Jimmy smile. "Oh really!? I like the sound of that. So what do you want to eat?" he asked.

"I would love to have some eggs if you have 'em."

"Well, let me go and see," he replied, and skipped off into the kitchen.

I heard the refrigerator door open. He waited a couple of seconds to speak. "Doesn't look like we got eggs. But we got milk and a box of cornflakes."

"What kind of milk is it?" I asked. I really didn't care about the type of milk that was in the refrigerator. My goal was to make conversation with him so he could feel comfortable talking to me. Being able to talk to me freely would begin to make him trust me.

"We drink one percent milk around here," he said, but then he paused. "Oh shoot, it's expired," he continued.

"It's okay," I told him.

I was indeed hungry. But cereal and milk definitely would have not done the job for me. I preferred not to eat anything else from this house. I hoped I'd be able to talk him into going back out to get me something to eat. If it worked, then I'd know for sure that his defenses could be broken.

"Hold up a minute, I found some pancake mix. And we got a half bottle of syrup," he said cheerfully. Boy, did he pop my balloon. But I couldn't let him get me while I was down. I came back and pretended to be allergic to syrup. "I can't eat syrup," I lied.

He rushed back into the TV room holding both the box of pancake mix and a bottle of syrup. "Why not?" he asked. He looked so disappointed. But I wasn't fazed by it. I was fighting for my life whether or not he realized it. So if it took me to shake up his emotions, then so the fuck what!

"I'm allergic," I finally said, giving him the most sincere expression I could muster.

"Ahhh, man, really?" he replied.

"Yep."

"Well, I guess I'm gonna have to think of something else to fix you."

"What about getting me a steak biscuit from McDonald's?" I suggested.

"But I can't leave you in the house while Mama is resting."

"She won't know." I tried to assure him.

"Oh no. Mama would kill me if she came out here and found out that I left you in here by yourself," he explained. And what was so bizarre about his explanation was that he went straight into child mode. I mean, he sounded just like a fucking nine-year-old kid. His mannerism and everything had taken me aback.

"Are you okay?" I asked him. At this very

moment he did not act like the man who kidnapped me against my will forty-eight hours ago.

"Yes. Of course I'm okay," he said, shaking the childlike disposition off. It was like he snapped out of it just like that.

"Are you sure you're okay?" I pressed the issue.

"Yeah. I'm good," he replied. He gave me the impression that he was trying to get a handle on his emotions. I didn't know whether to pry a little more or leave well-enough alone. This fucking guy was unstable, so I knew that the best thing for me to do was tread lightly.

"You know what? You're right. We don't want to upset your mama by you leaving me here alone. So let's think of something else to feed me," I added. I had to make him believe that he was right and that he was still in control.

"Okay. Yeah. Let's do that," he agreed.

He headed back into the kitchen and ended up making me several small pancakes. I told him to leave them plain instead of pouring syrup on top of them. Under normal circumstances I would've eaten a steak biscuit from McDonald's. Agent Sean would've had one of his flunkies around the safe house run out and fetch me the whole breakfast meal. I can't tell you how badly I wished I had not left that house. I never thought I'd say this, but I sure missed Agent Sean.

While this nutcase fed me the pancakes, I

began to pull out little intimate details about him. I needed to know who I was really dealing with. "How old are you?" I started off saying.

"How old do I look?" he asked me, and then he smiled. He was acting like we were playing a fucking guessing game. I wasn't trying to get to know him so we could be a couple. I just wanted to know if he had all his fucking marbles. But I allowed the chips to fall where they may and went along with his bullshit.

"You look like you're thirty-five."

"Nah, I'm forty-seven." He smiled once more.

"I hate to pry, but is that your real mother in the other room?"

"No, she's not. But she's had me since I was five years old."

"Did she adopt you?" I continued to question him.

"Yeah. She was my foster mother at first. And then after my fifth birthday she decided to keep me."

"Do you know what happened to your real mother?"

"No."

"Do you wish to know?"

"All I need is that lady in the other room. She took me when no one else would. So I owe her my life."

"Do you take medication?" I asked. I swear I didn't mean for that question to come out of my mouth.

He looked at me like I was crazy. I braced myself for what would happen next.

"No. I don't take pills," he answered me. He didn't seem upset by my question. "But Mama does give me vitamins and stuff."

"What kind of vitamins?" I probed.

"Just some vitamin C and iron pills."

"Oh, okay. That's good," I replied, trying to downplay the conversation. I didn't want him to blow my spot up by telling his mama I gave him the third degree. She was an old lady but she had more sense than I gave her credit for.

Mr. Psycho and I continued to chat about things that really didn't matter to me. So I had to continue reminding myself that my doing this would eventually win his trust and garner my freedom.

Now I wasn't naïve by a long shot. I knew that I would have a fight on my hands the day I managed to leave here. They're going to go for blood, but I will be up for the challenge, especially since my life will be on the line. I also needed to take into account that I may have to take their lives before I escape. As many dead bodies as I've seen, killing may become natural.

In my life there was never a dull moment.

Chapter 7

The Manhunt Continues

I was reluctant to let Agent Zachary ride with me to do another search for Lynise, but I decided to do it anyway. Agent Humphreys stayed back at the safe house while Agents Rome and Mann followed in a separate car.

"Thank you for letting me ride with you today," Zachary said.

"You don't have to thank me," I told her.

"I know I don't. But with everything that's going on, I appreciate you giving me the chance to make things right between you and me."

"It's no problem," I commented, and then I switched the topic of our conversation. "Wanna do some face-to-face investigating today?" I asked her. I needed to get a few people on board to help us find Lynise. See, Agent Zachary was a woman, and the good thing about her was that she didn't look like an agent. She'd be perfect to go undercover."

"I'll do whatever you need me to do," she told me.

Getting her to execute my plan meant we were one step away from perhaps finding Lynise. I thanked her for it.

"No need for that. That's what I am here for," she told me. I wanted to believe that she was being sincere, but I couldn't. Zachary was full of shit. She hated Lynise because she knew I fucked her and she knew that I had feelings for her. She'd railroad Lynise and hang her out to dry if she had her way. So anything that remotely sounded like she had Lynise's best interest at heart was pure bullshit!

It was eleven o'clock in the morning when we arrived in Norfolk. It was my idea to check out a few of the strip clubs. Club Diamonds was the first stop. Rome and I parked our cars at a Chinese restaurant directly across the street from the club. I instructed Zachary to go into the club and act like she was looking for a job. She was gamed for it. Before she exited the vehicle she removed her government-issued firearm and badge from her hip and left it on the car seat. "Just act natural," I told her.

"I got this," she said, and walked from the car.

While I watched Zachary as she walked toward the club, I noticed a couple of drug dealers standing next to their cars in the parking lot. Both guys were black. One was flashier than the other. The one that was less flashy had a few words for Zachary. I couldn't hear what he was saying, but from his expression I could tell that he was flirting with her. Zachary ignored him and continued on into the club. After the door closed behind her, I looked down at my watch to keep count of the time.

"Do you guys have visuals?" I radioed to Rome and Mann.

"Yes, we've got visuals," Agent Rome radioed back.

"Stay on guard," I instructed him.

"Roger that," he replied.

I watched the front door of the strip club from the time Agent Zachary walked inside until the time she came out. It took her a total of fifteen minutes. The two guys that were once in the parking lot had left. A black G-63 Mercedes Benz truck pulled up while Zachary exited the club. The truck stopped and then the window rolled down. "Do you guys see what I see?" I talked into the radio.

"Yes, we're locked in on the black SUV," Agent Rome answered.

"Can you see inside?" I asked.

"No. The tint is too dark," Rome replied.

"Neither can I. So let's just hang back and wait on her cue," I told him.

"Ten-four," Rome said, and then cut off communication.

I couldn't see the driver, but my guess was

that it was a man. My heart rate picked up while I watched Agent Zachary's body movements. She looked in my direction a couple of times, but she did it in a way to prevent the driver from looking my way.

After a few more words were exchanged, I saw a man's hand pass her a business card. She smiled at him and then she walked away from the truck. I radioed Agents Rome and Mann. "She's on the move," I said.

"We got a visual," Rome replied.

"Be on guard, fellows, because whoever is driving that vehicle hasn't exited it yet. So my guess is that she's being watched."

"Roger that," Rome added.

As Agent Zachary crossed the street, she looked directly at me. So I motioned for her to walk by my car and continue on into the restaurant. I had no idea who was in that SUV. But whoever it was took every precaution to conceal their identity. Thankfully, Agent Rome and I had parked our cars behind the cars of other patrons who were dining at the restaurant. If not, then our cover would've been blown.

After waiting for close to thirty minutes, the driver finally exited the SUV. He was a black male. He was tall, and he looked to be in his early forties. He was dressed casually. To sum it up, he definitely looked like new money.

Immediately after he went into the club, I called Zachary and told her to get her ass out of the restaurant. Seconds later, she scrambled to my car with a take-out container. Once she was inside the car, I pressed down on the accelerator and fled the scene. Agent Rome followed.

"You will not believe who I was just talking to," she started off saying.

"Who?" I said. I wasn't in the mood to play a guessing game. I wanted to get to the facts.

"I just met the Carter brothers' cousin Malik," she said. Hearing her utter the words *Carter brothers* was like music to my ears. How ironic was that? Was it fate that brought us here?

"You have got to be kidding, right?" I smiled. I was becoming anxious. It was like she wasn't coming out with the information fast enough. "Was he alone?" I wanted to know.

"Yes."

"Did he tell you why he was at the club? He is the owner?"

Zachary pulled his business card from her front pants pocket. "That's what his card says," she replied as she handed him the card.

I took a look at the business card. And there it was, printed in black ink: Malik Carter, owner and operator of the Club Diamonds. I got a chilling feeling looking at the card, so I handed it back to Zachary. "How do you know that he's the cousin?"

"Because he told me. He asked me if I ever heard of his two older cousins who own most of the businesses and strip clubs in the area."

"What did you say?"

"I told him that I hadn't. So he comes back and says that I must not be from around here, because everybody knows the Carter brothers."

"What did you tell him?"

"I told him I had just moved here from Philly and that I was looking for work. He wanted to know if I was a dancer. I told him no. But I did tell him that I wanted to be a waitress. And that's when he gave me his card and told me to call him later."

"Great job, Zachary! Great job," I commented.

I gathered all the agents together when we got back to the safe house. I gave Agent Zachary the floor so she could bring all the agents up to speed about her chat with the Carter brothers' cousin, Malik. After she filled them in on the details I stepped in and told them how we were going to put Zachary to work on the inside so she could gather all the intel we needed. I had a hunch that Lynise was in the area and hopefully by doing this, this would bring us closer to finding her.

Later that night, I picked up a throwaway phone from a nearby convenient store and got Agent Zachary to call this Malik character. We needed to get the ball rolling. When he answered his phone, Zachary put him on speaker. "Hi, is this Malik?"

"Yes, it is," we all heard him say.

"Hi, Malik, this is Priscilla," she lied. Priscilla was the name she had given him when she met him earlier in the parking lot of the strip club.

"It's good to hear your voice," he told her.

"Likewise."

"So you want a job, huh?"

"Yes. Are you going to hire me?"

"How badly do you want to work?" He pressed the issue.

"Well, I told you that I just moved to the area and that I was living at a relative's house. So the quicker I get a job, the better situated I can be."

"When can you start working?"

"I can start tomorrow."

"Of course you can. Just meet me at the club tomorrow night and we'll talk about the specifics."

"Okay. Well, I guess I'll see you then," she told him, and ended their call.

The minute after Agent Zachary hung up with the strip club owner, we put a plan in motion. "Listen, you guys, Agent Zachary is going to be our eyes and ears while she's waitressing at Club Diamonds. Every night one of us will go in the club and act as a patron so we can make sure that she's not in harm's way," I began to explain.

"Have you thought about how she is going to get there? You know she can't drive one of our undercover vehicles," Agent Humphreys pointed out.

"I made a call back to the office and they're getting things in motion so we can pick up a vehicle in this area by tomorrow," I explained.

"What about some new clothes?" Zachary asked me.

"I put in a request for that too. But while we're waiting for that to be approved, I'm gonna let you use the credit card I was issued for this trip."

"Are we gonna still continue on search missions while Zachary is working at the club?" Agent Mann wanted to know.

"Yes, we will still continue on with our search," I assured him. "Any other questions?" I asked, looking around at all the agents standing in a huddle.

"When you called headquarters, did you tell them that our witness had escaped?" Agent Rome asked.

"No, I didn't," I replied.

"Well, how did you explain you needing a car and an approval to buy a new wardrobe?" his questions continued.

I knew Rome was trying to fuck with me, but I let his bullshit roll off my back. "When you're the head of command you don't have to answer certain questions."

"So are you going to eventually tell them?"

"Yes, I will. And when I do, I'm gonna inform them that you were the cause of her escaping."

"What the fuck do you mean by that?" Agent

Rome roared. The veins near his temple nearly exploded.

"It is what it is, Rome. You and I both know that you had something to do with our witness escaping."

"That's bullshit! I'm not going to let you stick that one on me."

"I'm sorry, but it's already done. You did what you did, and that's final."

Agent Rome felt the heat falling down around him. So when it became unbearable, he charged at me. Luckily Agents Mann and Humphreys stopped him in his tracks. "I'm not gonna let you play me like I'm some kind of punk. And I'm not going to take the fall because you failed to do your job properly."

"Technically my job is to oversee you and the rest of the agents in this house. And while I was overseeing, I noticed that you were doing God knows what with my witness in the backyard of the house while it was pitch black. And up to this very moment, you still have not come up with a good-enough reason why that happened."

"I told you what happened. If you don't believe me, then it's on you," he commented sarcastically.

"Come on, you guys, we gotta break this up. We got a job to do and we won't be able to do it if we're at each other's neck," Agent Humphreys said.

Agent Rome and I retreated to opposite sides of the safe house. Agent Zachary accompanied me while Agent Rome sat downstairs with the rest of the agents. This separation did wonders for us.

I still looked at him like the snake he was.

Chapter 8

I Need to Get Out of Here

"Jimmy, aren't you supposed to be at work?" The old white lady asked after she entered the TV room. It was a few minutes after midnight.

"I'm off tonight, Mama," he replied, his eyes glued to the television, while I was still strapped down to the same fucking wheelchair like I was disabled. Jimmy's goofy-looking ass was sitting on the love seat only a few feet away from me.

We watched all the news stations around the clock. It was his mother's idea to stay informed. I'd eavesdropped on a couple of their conversations. It puzzled her to know that there hadn't been any missing person's reports on me. I knew it would blow their minds if they knew that I was under Witness Protection. And when you were under Witness Protection, every agent assigned to your case had to stay tight-lipped when it came to the witnesses.

"Has she been giving you any trouble?" she asked as she sat down on the other sofa.

"Oh no, Mama, she's been really good. That's why I didn't put the gag back around her mouth," he replied, refusing to take his eyes away from the TV.

"What's happening on the news? Anything new?" she continued to question him.

"Nah, nothing new. They just keep talking about the last two girls I killed."

"Have they found their bodies yet?" She seemed interested, as if they were playing some fucking hide-and-seek game.

"Nope. But they will if they keep searching Bay View Drive near the Ocean View beach."

"Okay, but don't forget that you dumped their bodies out there over two weeks ago and it's crab season. So when they do finally find them, their faces won't be recognizable because those blue crabs are going to disfigure them."

"Yeah, Mama, you're right. I didn't think about that," I heard him say. I was in total awe as I listened to these two talk about two innocent women's lives. They acted like cold-hearted ax maniacs. I had never seen anything like this before, even when I hung out in the hood. Niggas I knew that took someone else's life didn't sit around and talk about it like it was all fun and games. They killed the person and kept it moving. That's it.

"Any word on her?" she asked as she pointed in my direction.

"No, Mama. Nothing."

"That's strange," she commented.

I laughed to myself without even realizing it. Only for that moment, it felt like I had one up on them, even though I was being held against my will. I knew all along why they were watching all the news channels like a hawk. So for them to wonder about what was going on in my life that prevented my name from being plastered all over the TV made me feel like there was some hope for me.

"Hey, girl, where are you really from?"

"I'm from Newport News," I lied.

She gritted at me. "Are you lying to me?"

"No, ma'am," I lied once again.

"Well, why ain't nobody reported you missing?"

"I don't know."

"Oh, you know."

"I swear I don't."

"Mama, I believe she's telling the truth."

"Oh, shut up! You don't know what you're talking about. She could've been lying and you wouldn't even know it," the lady snapped.

"But Mama, I already told you where I picked her up from."

"Picking her up from Newport News doesn't mean that's where she lived. She's a whore, Jimmy. And whores travel from place to place."

"I am not a whore," I blurted out. This bitch really offended me. She didn't know shit about me. And if I hadn't been strapped to the chair, I would have closed her mouth permanently. It didn't matter that she was old. Old bitches can get smacked too.

"Mama, she is not a whore. She's a good girl." Jimmy tried to defend me.

"What time did you pick her up the other night?"

"Around this time."

"Well, there you go. Only whores hang out on the streets this time of night."

"I was only on the streets that time of night because my car broke down," I lied. I had to think of something, even if it was a lie, to prove to her that I wasn't a ho.

"I don't believe that for one minute."

"Mama, can you please be nice to her?" Jimmy pouted like a child.

"I will be nice to her after she tells us the truth."

"But what if she's already telling us the truth?"

"Oh, Jimmy, get the stick out of your ass. I can see that this girl doesn't have an ounce of honesty in her body from a mile away. She is just like all the other girls you brought home."

"Mama, no, she's not. She's special." Jimmy defended me once again. This time he got up from the chair and immediately embraced me. The feeling of his touch made my skin crawl. But I couldn't show the emotions, because his mother was watching my every move.

"Mama, she's different from the rest of them," Jimmy continued, and then he kissed me on my forehead. Right then and there, I wanted to jump out of my skin. His kiss was wet and it felt disgusting. But I held on to my composure. I had to. I had to prove that everything this lady was saying about me was wrong. It was hard to do. But I was making it work.

"Oh, bologna!" she replied, and then she blew us off with a hand gesture.

Thankfully Jimmy didn't hold me in his arms too long. After he diffused the conversation about me, he let me go and headed back to his seat.

Everything became quiet for the next ten minutes, until one of the local news stations reported an Amber Alert, which was a child abduction. We all tuned into the broadcast. The report lasted about a minute and a half. And when it was over, the old lady had something to say. "I betcha the mama's boyfriend had something to do with that little girl being kidnapped."

"It would be a shame if that were true," Jimmy added.

"Yeah, it sure would. I just don't understand why grown-ups won't pick on someone their size. Leave the children alone. They're innocent."

"So you're against adults abducting kids?" I blurted out. I couldn't hold my words back. I had to put this old bitch in the hot seat.

"Oh, absolutely," she replied confidently.

"Well, why is it okay for your son to kidnap innocent women? I mean, women are at a disadvantage if you put them next to a man. Am I right?" I continued. This bitch was making me go there with her ass.

"Are you getting smart with me, young lady?" she snapped.

"No. I just wanna know why it's not okay to kidnap a kid but it's okay to kidnap a woman."

Jimmy's mother got to her feet and started walking toward me. Jimmy jumped to his feet too and stood between his mother and me. That didn't stop her from spitting fire at my ass. She released the fury. "Don't you ever question me again about what is right and what's wrong," she spat, as she waved fingers at me. "Women have done my son wrong for years. They played on his feelings and mistreated him. And they used him for as long as I can remember. So sure, it's okay for him to do anything he wants to do to women. They deserve everything that comes their way because they are manipulative, greedy, spiteful, and they don't care about anyone but themselves."

"I'm not like that. I'm a good person." I choked up listening to this fucking lady telling me how women were. But I wasn't like that. When I worked at the strip club as the bartender, life back then was good to me. I worked and I minded my business. I also had a best friend who ended up turning against me because of a heartless-ass nigga. Now the both of them are dead. And the nigga who killed them wants me dead. So again, I was a good person until my world fell down around me. The person who I am now is only trying to stay alive long enough to maybe draw social security one of these days. That was it.

"Oh, get out of here with those meaningless tears," she commented, and then she turned back around and sat in her seat.

Jimmy leaned over toward me and wiped the teardrops from my face with the backs of his hands. He seemed bothered by my tears. "Mama, you made her upset."

"She ain't crying for real. She's putting on an act," she replied sarcastically.

Unbeknownst to either of them, I was crying because of where my life's choices had taken me. I was ready for a change. But this wasn't the change I had hoped for.

Jimmy's dumb ass finally got his mother to settle down. They rambled on for at least another twenty minutes. But nothing they said even made sense. I drifted off to sleep a couple of times, but they always seemed to find a way to break my sleep.

"Mama, you know I love you, right?"

"Yes, baby. I know you do."

"And you know I'll never stop loving you, right?"

She chuckled. "Of course I know that, silly."

"Well, won't you stop giving Pam a hard time? I know you don't trust her. But something in my heart is telling me that she's the one. So just give her a chance."

The old lady paused for a second and then she said, "I'll tell you what. I'll back off of her until I see different. But you gotta promise me that you'll never let her come between what you and I have. Do you understand?"

"Yes, Mama. I understand," I heard him say, and then their chat ended.

I sat there in that fucking wheelchair wearing three-day-old clothes and had not bathed once. So to hear this fool act like he and I were going to live happily ever after was a fucking joke to me. I'd have killed myself before I lay down and fucked this pervert. This fucking grease ball and his mother were going to be in for a rude awakening.

Reality was about to set in.

Chapter 9

Treading on Thin Ice

Agent Zachary and I went to the mall to purchase a few clothing items so she could start the waitress job at Club Diamonds that night. We headed to Patrick Henry Mall, which was the nearest mall to the safe house. We shopped at several stores and came out with a few sexy, form-fitting blouses and dark-colored tights. Once she felt she had enough things to go undercover, we headed back to the safe house. On the way there Agent Zachary wanted to talk about ways to smoothly navigate through her first night of this undercover work. I could sense that she was extremely nervous. "You know you're gonna be fine, right?"

"Yes."

"So why the long face?"

"Have you thought about who's going to accompany me tonight?"

"I'm gonna be with you tonight so I can feel the place out."

"Are you gonna be there the entire night?"

"No. I'm gonna go in a few minutes before you get there. And then when you get off, I'll be watching your back from a block away. That way I can follow you back to the safe house."

"Thank you. I appreciate you making sure that I'm okay."

"That's what I am here for," I told her.

"Do you think we're gonna find Lynise through this channel? Because remember, there is a huge bounty on her head. So if it were me, I wouldn't hang out at a strip club owned by a close relative of the men who want me dead."

"I totally agree with you. But look at it this way, even if Lynise never shows her face at that club, there could still be some buzz going around about where she is. I just want you to keep your eyes and ears open. That's it."

"How do you want me to handle that Malik guy, because you know he's gonna be making passes at me. You heard him in action when I put him on speaker yesterday."

"Just try to keep it clean. Let him know that you have boundaries and that he needs to respect you."

"What if that doesn't work?"

"It will work. Women always have the power.

But most of you give up so easily, because you got to have a man."

Zachary chuckled. "You are so right. And now that I think about it, I know a lot of women who do it."

"If y'all would just stand your ground, you'd have the world eating out of your hands."

"I wish it were that easy."

"It can be," I assured her.

Back at the safe house I laid down a couple of rules before we headed out. The main concern I had was for her to understand that her safety came first. "Don't try to be tough," I instructed her. "And don't try to be a hero. You aren't there for that. Someone will always be around to step in if something goes south. So just relax and get as much information as you can until I pull you off this detail," I continued.

"What if I see someone dealing drugs? Am I supposed to turn my head?"

"First of all, we're out of our jurisdiction. So of course I want you to turn your head. We are only here to find Lynise. Anything outside of that does not concern us," I replied.

"What if someone gets killed?"

"Now, that's different. But again, let's try to keep your involvement in the club to a minimum. We don't have a lot of time left to find our witness, so let's stay focused. The quicker we can get intel, the quicker we can get out of there."

"Okay. I think I can manage that."
"Good. So, let's get started."

Club Diamonds was packed from wall to wall with drug-dealing thugs. From the outside the club looked cheesy. On the inside the decor was suitable for the mixed crowd that was spending money tonight. There were a few white men. But there were more black men sitting around the stage. I even noticed a couple of black women throwing single dollar bills at the exotic dancers. There were five big, black bouncers in the club. Two stood at the front door, one stood near the bar area, and the other two stood on the opposite ends of the stage. They were definitely in position to do damage control if need be.

While I checked out my surroundings, and the dancers of course, Agent Zachary came strolling into the club. Our eyes met briefly before she turned her attention to the woman standing behind the bar. I couldn't make out what was being said, but after the bartender got the attention of the bouncer standing next to the bar, I figured out that she needed to be escorted to another part of the club. They both disappeared behind the stage. I sat there patiently with a Corona in hand and waited to see what would happen next. Five minutes passed and there was no sign of Zachary. Then ten minutes passed and there was still no Zachary.

But after waiting a couple more minutes Agent Zachary finally reappeared with the bouncer walking behind her. I let out a sigh of relief that all was well.

I allowed her to get in the groove of things before I asked her to come and take a drink order from me. I wanted to make sure we didn't look suspicious talking to each other. "I got worried when you went behind the stage with the bouncer," I told her.

"He had to take me to the back office to see Malik."

"So, he's here?"

"Yes, he's here."

"That's shocking, because I didn't see his SUV outside."

"He's probably driving something else."

"So, what did he say?"

"Nothing but that he's glad to see me. And that he wants me to come back and see him before I leave for the night."

"Was he alone?"

"Yeah, he's alone. He was on a call when the bouncer and I walked into his office."

"Well, you be careful."

"I will," she said. But before she walked off she added, "Let me get you something else to drink so we don't stick out like sore thumbs."

I smiled. "Yeah, why don't you do that."

Just like I had planned, I left the strip club and hung out in my car until Zachary ended her shift. I waited in my car for almost three hours before Zachary walked out the front door. It was two-thirty in the morning, to be exact. And she wasn't alone. A short, Hispanic-looking woman walked alongside Zachary, but then they parted ways. The woman got into a white Range Rover Sport. She beeped her horn at Zachary as she drove out of the parking lot. Zachary got into the Toyota Camry our department head approved for her. I waited a few minutes before I followed her back to the safe house. I had to make sure she wasn't being followed. And when I realized that she wasn't, I followed suit.

Agent Zachary arrived back at the safe house before I did. When I walked into the house she was sitting in the kitchen telling Agent Humphreys how her night went. "It was only a Thursday night and I raked in one hundred thirty-two dollars in tips."

"That's awesome," he told her.

"Tell me about it."

"I see you like your new job," I interjected.

She smiled. "It wasn't half bad," she replied.

"Did you get a chance to talk to your boss again?" I questioned her.

"No. As a matter of fact, he got a call and left the club in a rush."

"Did anyone say why he left in such a rush?"

"No. No one said anything about it. Everybody pretty much minds their own business."

"Well, who was that woman you walked out the club with?"

"Her name is Camille. She's one of the other waitresses at the club."

"Did she tell you how long she's been working there?"

"Yeah, she said she's been there almost six months now."

"Did she say anything negative about the club?"

"All she said was for me to watch out for the other women in the club because they are shady."

"That's it?"

"Yep. That's it."

"Well, I'm sure there's more to her story. So just keep your eyes and ears open. And good job on your first day."

"I will. And thank you," she said.

I sat back and watched Zachary exit the kitchen. I could tell how important I made her feel when I acknowledged that she had done a good job. Agent Humphreys noticed it too. "Everyone knows that she has a sweet spot for you," he commented.

"Is it that obvious?" I asked.

"Come on, buddy. Everyone in this house knows about her feelings for you. She will do anything you ask her to do. No questions asked," Agent Humphreys continued.

"I know," I said, and then I paused.

"Don't get quiet now," Humphreys joked. "The damage is done."

I sighed heavily. "Don't remind me," I finally

said. It was exhausting thinking about how I fucked up and slept with Agent Zachary. Agent Humphreys was right, Zachary was sticking her neck out only because of her feelings for me.

"So, how do you think this undercover work is going?" He changed the subject.

"So far, so good."

"Have you thought about how long we're gonna work that detail?"

"I'm thinking maybe a couple weeks," I replied. But I wasn't too sure. I honestly didn't know how long we were going to work the strip club detail. At this moment, I was desperate to try anything to find Lynise.

"Have you decided when you're going to call headquarters to let them know about what is going on?" Humphreys probed.

"Yeah, I figured if we didn't find Lynise in the next couple of days, then I would let them know. That way we can get more agents to join forces with us."

"Foster, you know I'm going to always have your back. But I think that you're going about this thing wrong. We should've called headquarters immediately after our witness escaped."

Agent Humphreys poked holes at my decision not to report Lynise's escape to headquarters. All egos aside, I had to admit that Humphreys was right. I should've reported the incident to our acting director. But I felt it was necessary for me not to because Joyce, who was the head of our department, was just murdered. It was blatantly obvious that we have a mole in our department. I needed to find out who it was before I gave them that sensitive information. I was not about to let anyone breach my operation. After Lynise is found, we will move her to another secured location and move forward with our investigation to lock Bishop's drug-dealing and murdering-ass up.

I swear I couldn't wait to see that day.

Chapter 10

Who's Really in Charge?

"**W**ould you please let me wash up? I've been sitting in this wheelchair for four days. I know y'all have smelled me by now," I complained. It was nine-thirty in the morning, and I was falling deeper into depression. The foul smell coming from my body was becoming unbearable.

"My mama doesn't think it's a good idea to leave you in the bathroom."

"But you leave me in the bathroom to piss!" I snapped. I couldn't be more disgusted with these people.

"I know. But it's gonna take you more time to bathe. And she's afraid that you may try to escape," he tried to whisper.

"Escape and go where? I will be naked, for God's sake," I reasoned.

"I understand that you're upset. But you're gonna have to calm down before she comes in here."

"I'm tired of calming down. I need you to stand up for me," I said. I knew this would be a great time to try to get into Jimmy's head. His mother had a stronghold on him. She controlled everything about him. So while she was in her bedroom with the door closed, I decided to try to chip away at some of the damage she had done to him. But before I could open my mouth she walked into the room. My plans were crushed. She looked directly at me. "Do you have something to say to me?" she asked.

I choked up. I wanted to say something, but my mouth wouldn't move. I wasn't scared or anything. I guess I was a bit surprised that she heard me talking to her lunatic of a son. I braced myself because I knew her wrath was about to be unleashed.

"I just want to wash my ass!" I yelled.

Within a blink of an eye, this bitch lunged and swung at me. "Don't you ever talk to me like that again!" she roared.

Luckily Jimmy stopped her from hitting me. "Well, let me wash up," I yelled back. I wasn't backing off from this damn lady. I needed to put her in her place. She and her son had violated me enough.

"I'm not letting you do a damn thing. Now sit in that seat and shut up before I make you regret the day you were born, missy." Her voice sounded demonic now.

"My name ain't Missy. It's Lynise," I replied, seeming irritated. But my reaction to all this madness didn't matter. What mattered was that I had just told these two nutjobs my real name. I was caught red-handed. Jimmy's expression turned from concern to shock. Everything seemed to happen in slow motion after he turned his attention toward me. His mother stood beside him and watched him as he became enraged. "So, your name isn't Pam? It's Lynise," he said, gritting his teeth.

"No, Pam is my middle name," I managed to say. I knew I had to keep this lie going. But it didn't work. Jimmy grabbed my neck and began to squeeze the breath out of me. I coughed while gasping for air. "You fucking lied to me!" he snapped. "My mother was right. You are just like those other girls. I fucking hate you!"

"Son, I told you she was not to be trusted. I told you," she chimed in.

Jimmy continued to hold a death grip around my neck as the pressure from his hand seemed to take life from me by the second. I could see death in his eyes as his mother applauded his efforts to kill me. It was apparent that she wanted me dead more than he did. She got her rocks off seeing me struggle for my life. This bitch was more sinister than the devil himself. It can't get any worse than that.

After Jimmy crippled me for what seemed like a lifetime, I started slipping out of consciousness. And all I could think about was that I was going to end up like his last two victims. The difference between us was that I had no one looking for me but U.S. Marshals and federal agents.

When it felt as if I was about to take my last breath, Jimmy released his hand from my neck. I was still coughing. "What are you doing? Kill her!" I heard his mother yell as I dropped my head low.

I closed my eyes and thought back on the time when my life was good. I was in love with Duke before he turned into a fucking monster. He used to be so nice and sweet. He was a gentleman at heart, especially the night he took me to his condo in the Cosmopolitan building and told me he wanted me to live there so he could take care of me.

The condo was decorated in an art deco style with all the furniture having that ultramodern look. However, one thing struck me as strange. Looking around the condo, I didn't notice any photographs or signs that the house was his. Even stranger, I noticed the same thing at his other house—just expensive artwork on the walls and every type of high-priced electronic gadget you could imagine. I started wondering why none of Duke's homes were personalized with little signs of him. No shoes lying around, no pictures, nothing that said he lived at either location. I looked at his fine ass and quickly put my paranoid thoughts out of my mind. I wasn't trying to drive myself crazy thinking negative thoughts about Duke. I decided to go with the flow when it came to him.

"Be right back," I remembered him saying.

"Where are you going?" I'd asked him.

"To get you and me something to drink," he'd said, and then he disappeared.

When Duke disappeared to get the drinks I looked down at the magazines on the coffee table and flipped through a few of them. I remembered scanning *GQ* and *Essence* before I noticed copies of *Woman's Health* and *Vogue* magazines. My face crinkled at that the sight of the women magazines. *Why would a single man have copies of girly magazines?* Girly magazines that weren't porn. Duke surely didn't look like the type to read that kind of material. I heard Duke's footsteps so I'd hurriedly put the women's magazines back under the pile. That shit was bothering me, but I wouldn't have dared questioned him. I was nowhere near that status with him yet, but I surely did make a mental note to myself.

Immediately after he gave me my drink, he sat beside me and we'd started talking about his real estate investments. Then he told me how he loved kids and wanted to eventually open up a free clinic for children. I'd thought his gesture was so nice. It really warmed my heart. Duke could tell that I was really into him that night, because a few minutes later he'd placed his hand behind my head. I closed my eyes as he ran his fingers through my naturally long hair. I remember wanting to open my mouth to say something, but Duke quickly stuck his tongue inside of it. He kissed me passionately.

Duke pressed himself against me, and I felt his throbbing dick against my pelvis. I began grinding my hips upward toward his dick, trying to press my clit on his rock-hard shit. I'd wanted him to know that I wanted to feel him inside of me real bad. Duke lifted my shirt and with one touch he had the front clasp on my bra loosened. He had skills. My C-cup breasts jumped loose, and Duke put his mouth on my nipples. The heat from his mouth was sending me over the top. He sucked on my nipples so hard, he caused me to grind harder and faster. It felt so good, I had to move my head side to side. Each time I moved, Duke sucked harder and harder. I couldn't control myself.

My pussy became soaking wet. I felt the moisture in my panties. Duke stood up abruptly and hovered over me. I looked up at him with innocent eyes. He quickly unbuttoned my jeans, then pulled them down over my hips and all the way off. The cool air on my clit made me feel hot as hell. I spread my legs open so Duke could get a good look at my creamy pussy. Any inhibitions I'd had previously about sleeping with him early were gone.

One thing that stuck out in my head from that night was when I started fingering my pussy while Duke watched. He'd acted like he was more into that than I was, and I loved the attention. I saw the print of his dick clear as day. He saw me staring at it, so he grabbed it and rubbed his hands against it. Moments later, he dropped to his knees in front of me and put his face between my legs. He ate my pussy with so much poise. But things didn't end there, because after I had my first orgasm, Duke got up and slid out of his jeans. His legs were so toned, and his dick hung almost to his knees. I licked my lips, but before I could go down on him Duke hoisted me up and held me against him. I put my legs up around his waist and straddled him. I held on to his neck so I wouldn't fall while he guided his dick into my pussy. I bit my bottom lip when he put his thick, solid dick inside me before he flopped back on the couch. This time I rode him like a horse. I bounced up and down on his dick so hard he started breathing like he had just run a few laps around the block.

I bent over at the waist and pumped up and down on his dick again. Duke slapped my ass cheeks as I fucked the shit out of him. I planted my feet for leverage and then I used both of my hands and spread my ass cheeks apart so he could see his dick go in and out of my pussy. That was what we women live for—to drive a muthafucka crazy tapping that ass. The ultimate in pussy whipping.

I started to feel myself about to cum because the shaft of his dick was pressing on my G-spot. I sat up, closed my legs together, and squeezed his dick with my pussy. I remembered Duke bucking and screaming, so I knew he was about to cum too. Without saying a word, I jumped up quickly, allowing some of the cum from his dick to drip out of me, and then I turned around and he started jerking the rest of his cum onto my tits.

I remembered him telling me that he had never been fucked like that. I smiled and winked my eye at him. That was a compliment in my mind. I felt like I couldn't be replaced, but I was wrong. *Look at where I was now!*

Chapter 11

Snakes in the Grass

I assigned Agent Humphreys to accompany Agent Zachary on her third day at the strip club. While they were gone I decided to take the other car and ride around a bit. I took Lynise's file with me just in case I needed it. Time was of the essence, and it was running out.

I drove around the city of Virginia Beach. But I concentrated on the neighborhoods that were documented in her file. My agents and I had already searched this area, but I felt there were a few rocks that still hadn't been turned over.

After scouring the urban neighborhoods of Virginia Beach, I threw in the towel and headed back to the safe house. It was close to ten P.M., so

I stopped by a Chinese spot about two miles from the safe house. I ordered vegetable fried rice, paid the Asian woman behind the counter, and when she handed me my food, I thanked her and left.

Upon my return to the safe house I found nothing out of the ordinary except that Agents Rome and Mann weren't downstairs in the meeting room watching TV, which was where they generally hung out.

Once I put my food down on the kitchen table, I went to look for them to let them know that I had come back. I went upstairs to the second floor. And when I reached the top step I heard voices coming from the bedroom that Agent Mann was assigned to when we first got here. One of the voices was Agent Mann's and the other voice was Agent Rome's. I heard some laughter, and then I heard Lynise's name come up. So instead of letting them know that I had come back, I tiptoed as close as I could to the bedroom door to hear what was being said.

"Foster is really in over his head with this operation," I heard Agent Rome say.

"I told you we need to call headquarters and let them know what's going on," Agent Mann said.

"You know we can't go over his head. The acting director would crucify our asses if we did that," Agent Rome added.

"Not if we tell them that there's a bounty on her head," Agent Mann said.

"You may have a point there. But remember, the fewer agents we have looking for her, the harder it'll be to find her. And the longer she's on the streets, the more likely it is that someone will see her and take her ass out. And when that happens, she'll never be able to blow our cover," Agent Rome pointed out.

"Yeah, you're right. And we can't have that."

"No. We can't have that." I heard Rome sigh.

"So what are we going to do moving forward?"

"We'll just continue to act like we're looking for her. And who knows, maybe one day soon we'll see on the news that someone has collected on her bounty."

Agent Mann found humor in what Rome said and burst into laughter.

I, on the other hand, didn't find any of that bullshit they said funny. We're supposed to have one another's back, especially in this line of work. So to hear this joker telling his partner that they're going against me was fucked up. And what could Lynise know about those fucking creeps? What could be so damaging that they wanted to feed her ass to the dogs? Whatever it was, I was going to find out about it. But until then, I was going to hold my composure and act like I'd never heard any of that shit. Knowing that these motherfuckers were snakes made me look at them totally different. They honestly could not be trusted, which brought me to the decision that I was going to have to tell someone about this. But who? Was I going to be able to trust Agent Zachary with this information? Or would it be in my best interest to tell only Agent Humphreys? I was really on the fence about this situation because I couldn't have another episode like the Norfolk Police Precinct blowing up.

I remembered yelling and telling everyone at the Third Precinct to get down after the building shook. It had felt like a fucking earthquake. Lynise fell to the floor first. Then Agent Rome and I dropped to the floor too. I ordered Lynise to stay low. Agent Zachary and the other agents did the same. But moments later, gunshots had rung out throughout the one-story building. The place was huge, and it had plenty of hallways and rooms.

The shooting had been nonstop. The conference room had two doors on the same side of the room, about thirty feet from each other. When the first door opened, two of my agents and two detectives turned their weapons toward the door as if on instinct.

"Don't shoot!" Agent Zachary had stated. "It's only me and Agent Carr."

"What the fuck is happening out there?" I asked them.

"Someone threw several grenades through the front door and they went off," Agent Zachary answered. She was panting. "And there's at least five or six gunmen that I counted emptying out their arsenal on every police officer they see," she'd continued. She looked spooked. She had acted as if she was out of her element.

"How far are they from this room?" I asked.

"If we get out of here now, we'll have at least a two-minute head start on them," she told me.

"Is there a back way out of this building?" I'd asked the detectives.

"Yeah, but there are a lot of hallways in this fucking building," Detective Whitfield responded. "The best way is to just keep heading toward the back and watch out for the hallways that lead to the front of the building."

"In other words, you guys are saying that if we don't watch our asses, we could still get blown away?" I replied.

Before he or Detective Rosenberg could respond, I'd grabbed Lynise's arm and said, "Time to move. Let's get out of here."

Agent Zachary was the first out the door since she was the closest to it. Lynise and I were next, and then Agent Rome and the other agents followed. But before we could hit the next hallway, three guys had come around the corner, and before they let off one shot, I'd pushed Lynise to the floor and every agent with me fired their weapons simultaneously. A couple of minutes later, Detectives Rosenberg and Whitfield came out of the conference room and fired shots of their own. "They have on flak vests!" Detective Whitfield screamed at us. "Shoot them in the face or below the groin if you can."

Finally all three guys were gunned down. Blood covered their entire bodies.

"Come on, let's get out of here!" Agent Rome yelled. In uniform order, all of us scrambled down the long hallway that led to another hallway that finally led to the back door of the precinct.

As we approached the back door, two more shooters had shot around the corner and started gunning at us like we were in a war. "Kick the door open!" I'd yelled. While Agent Zachary kicked at the door, the other agents started firing another set of rounds at the men who were pursuing us. Miraculously we made it out the back door before any of us were hit.

Everyone climbed into the SUVs and sped out of the precinct parking lot. One by one all the agents followed me. Engines were revved up and then we sped off like NASCAR drivers. "Agents take cover!" I remembered yelling from the window. "Lynise, you get down on the floor," I recalled telling her as we fled the scene.

The moment had arrived after we bolted out of the underground tunnel. It seemed like every thug in the area had the precinct surrounded. Mercenaries dressed in black had come from all angles, and they were busting shots at us like it was the Fourth of July.

Pop! Pop! Pop! Ping! Ping! Ping! Sounds of bullets hitting the SUV rattled my brain. If we hadn't had bulletproof windows, we'd have been in a world of trouble. So in my mind I knew I had been the one responsible for the Carter brothers and their assassins gunning at us on I-64. If I'd objected to those local cops interrogating Lynise, then the whole thing would not have happened.

Luckily my agents and I used precise judgment and extreme force to get out of this dangerous high-speed chase. A few cars crashed into each other while we forced our way ahead.

I vividly recalled the tunnel directly in front of us, right before the bridge that connected to Hampton. And as soon as we exited the tunnel, all hell broke loose.

A tall Latino, sporting dark sunglasses with his hair pulled back into a ponytail, had a bazooka in his hands and aimed directly at us. He pulled the trigger, and I knew we were dead, but suddenly Agent Rome veered left and the blast passed us and hit the SUV directly behind us. The impact was deadly, I was sure. Meanwhile, we had done a complete 360-degree turn, probably two times, before we finally stopped. Agents Rome and I jumped out of the car and joined the Latino and Agent Zachary and Carr. Agent Sean had told me to get out of the car and hide behind one of the cars. There was another black SUV, and I assumed it was the Latino's ride.

I'd instructed Lynise to hide behind one of the SUVs while all five agents were loaded for bear with some serious weapons. They all had assault rifles and handguns. The blast had taken out one SUV, and more thugs in a white sedan had run into the back of that vehicle.

The four doors of the SUV opened simultaneously as if they were synchronized. Four guys—two blacks, a white, and an Asian—came out blazing, but this was the shortest firefight in the history of firefights. It was as if every one of my agents had selected their own gunmen to kill. The four assholes went down fast.

When the massacre had finally ended, it was apparent that the Carter brothers and Bishop really wanted Lynise dead. And if they had to send a hundred mercenaries to do it, so be it. I knew that my agents and I would have to put our heads together so that incident wouldn't happen again.

Chapter 12

Fuel to the Fire

After Jimmy almost choked the life out of me, he stormed off to another part of the house. His mother sat in the chair across from me and made a bunch of snide remarks after I fully regained consciousness. My neck was so sore it was hard to swallow even saliva. "My son is gonna listen to me one of these days," she started off.

"All of you girls are nothing but harlots. You walk around here with your miniskirts and tight pants acting like the world belongs to you. I keep telling my boy that all you girls want to do is use him for whatever y'all can get. But guess what? It's not happening anymore. My son is going to give every last one of you what you deserve. And as long as I'm here, I'm gonna make sure it's done."

I sat there and listened to that crazy-ass lady run her mouth nonstop. I was too weak to feed into her shit. Her son just damn near killed me, so I needed to regroup. I lowered my head and cried myself to sleep.

While asleep I dreamt about the time Bishop started changing. I remembered one morning being awakened by his numerous telephone conversations and instead of getting up to start my day I'd lain there and eavesdropped. The first call I heard him make had to be to Keisha, because he sure did a lot of explaining about why he hadn't answered his phone when she called. The second call he made I assumed was to one of his employees, because I heard him literally spit fire through the receiver and threaten the person that if they hadn't taken care of what he instructed them to do, then it was going to be their ass on the chopping block. During that conversation he also instructed that person to go back and make sure they did a thorough cleaning. "Yo I swear, if that spot isn't squeaky clean, then we're gonna have some major fucking problems!" Bishop roared through the phone. "And the next time you wanna talk to me, don't call me on this phone. Hit me up on the throw-away phone," he continued, and then he ended the call.

Several minutes later, I heard him make another phone call. But that call lasted only sixty seconds. And before I realized it, Bishop had burst into the bedroom and startled the hell out of me. He literally stood over top of me and had screamed like his damn mind was going bad. I opened my eyes and saw the anger in his face. He'd been really angry with me that morning for touching his fucking cell phone.

"I tried to wake you up," I recalled saying to him. Unfortunately for me, my explanation didn't work. Bishop was not letting the matter go. He felt the need to chastise me because I caught his ass in the wrong. Not only that, it took the spotlight off him from the night before when I'd caught his ass standing outside the apartment talking and grinning from ear to ear with his new chick.

Unable to go back to sleep after Bishop's tirade, I'd grabbed my Blackberry from the nightstand and dialed Bria's number. I needed someone to talk to about Bishop's fucking anger issues. And who better to talk to than his sister Bria. She knew him longer than I did, so there was no question in my mind that she could give me some pointers as to how to handle him the next time he went on a rampage. Unfortunately she didn't answer her phone. I didn't know it then, but I later found out that Bishop had already did her in. I swear, if I had known that, I would've left him alone, packed up my things, and run for my life.

Or I could've run off with Sean after I met

him in the parking lot of the apartments we were living in at the time. Too bad, he was an undercover agent and not a cat really trying to get with me. It seemed like it was yesterday when I saw him. I recall walking toward my silver Jaguar. He broke his neck to speak to me after he stepped out of his sky blue big-boy Chevy Tahoe. He was dark skin and handsome like I like my men. Plus, he was the right height for me. He resembled Idris Elba. But he wasn't as fine as the actor.

I smiled and waved at him as I made my way toward my vehicle. Normally when we see each other, it's always in passing and Bishop was with me, so we would speak to each other and keep it moving. But for some reason I guessed he wasn't trying to let me get out of his sight without saying a few words to me since Bishop was nowhere around.

I didn't know much about Agent Sean except that he had just moved into the apartment three doors down from me a couple weeks earlier. I hadn't seen too much foot traffic to his place since he had moved in, so I was forced to believe he was either single or gay.

He'd walked toward me with the biggest smile he could muster up. I looked at him from head to toe and believe me, he'd looked really damn good rocking a pair of khaki cargo shorts, a white Lacoste polo, and a pair of brown, signature Louis Vuitton sneakers. On the surface, he looked like he was a hustler. But after he'd opened his mouth, he gave me the impression that he was educated. He was intriguing to say the least.

"Leaving without me?" he'd said jokingly.

We stopped within a couple feet from each other. "It looks that way," I replied, and then I smiled.

"Where's your man?" he pressed on.

"Where's your woman?" I threw the question back at him.

"If I had one she'd be with me right now." He smiled. "But it's not about me, it's about you. So answer the question."

"I'm not sure. But I'm sure that wherever he is, he's fine."

"Well, where are you headed?"

"Out to get a breakfast sandwich. Why?"

"Maybe because I would like to tag along."

"I don't think my man would like me driving another man around in a car he's paying for."

"Oh no, I was going to follow you in my truck."

I'd hesitated for a second to think about Sean's offer. While the idea of our having breakfast together sounded good, the chances of Bishop or someone who knew him seeing us dining out in a restaurant didn't sit well with me. It would be disastrous.

Then after it had dawned on me how Bishop was playing me with this new bitch named Chrissy, my whole perspective changed. Shit!

Why not have breakfast with this handsome gentleman? It wasn't as if we're going to check into a hotel. One harmless breakfast date wasn't going to hurt anyone.

"Come on, let's go," I'd instructed him.

"Where are we going?" he wanted to know.

"To the nearest breakfast diner."

"Well, I know this spot on the other side of the city, so follow me," he'd insisted.

"Okay. Let's do it then," I'd replied, and then I headed to my car.

I followed Sean to an all-day breakfast spot called Tops Diner on Passaic Avenue. Immediately after he parked his truck, he rushed over to my car, opened the door, and held it open so I could step out. "Thank you," I said.

Minutes after we entered the diner we were seated at a table near a window. The restaurant wasn't busy, so we were able to get our food very quickly. I had chicken and waffles, while he dug into a Colorado omelet.

In the beginning, he and I made small talk. I gave him some of my backstory of where I was from and my educational background. When he asked me how Bishop and I met, I stretched the truth a bit. I told him Bishop and I met at a strip club back in Virginia, which was partially the truth. I failed to tell him Bishop only came to Virginia to avenge his brother's death and the real reason why I followed him to New Jersey. I was sure if I had told him about all the murder and mayhem that happened back in Virginia, he would've ended our breakfast date in the blink of an eye.

I wasn't on *America's Most Wanted,* but I had some bad history that no one needed to know about. And I wasn't stupid enough to share that kind of information. Even if Agent Sean was the bad-boy type, no way I was sharing information I had tucked in the back of my head and would carry to the grave. No one in their right mind would admit any wrongdoing or the fact that they were on the run from the police. So I'd continued to smile and act like I was Ms. Goody Two-shoes, not knowing that he was a government agent.

I remembered that halfway through breakfast he became flirtatious and I'd loved every minute of it. After he'd told me he was twenty-nine years old and had just graduated from Penn State, I was really impressed.

"So, what do you do for a living?" I pressed on.

He'd smiled shyly. "I'm kind of between jobs right now," he admitted.

"Well, how do you pay your bills?" I wanted to know.

Something inside me said he was slinging some type of narcotic. I always had an eye for a street hustler, and he had the look to a tee. And most often when a guy worked on the street, he had a certain mannerism. Meaning, he would cut his money with his back facing the person in front of him, he would talk in code while he was on the phone, and he would always look over his shoulder.

While he and I ate, he looked around checking out our surroundings at least ten times, if not more. That kind of behavior had drug dealer written all over it, but how was I to judge? I felt as if those were the only men I attracted, so I figured why fight it or try to change it.

Immediately after he'd told me that his parents were well off and that they sent him money to pay his bills, I kind of took it with a grain of salt and said whatever. At that point it really didn't matter. I figured the less I knew about him, the better off I'd be. Besides, at the end of the day, how he got his money was his business, not mine.

"So, how many kids do you have running around here?" I asked him.

"One. I've got a seven-year-old son named after me."

"That's cool. Where is he?"

"He lives with his mother down south."

"Down south, where?

"Atlanta, Georgia. His mother moved there about a year ago to take care of her mother after her father passed."

"I'm sorry to hear that."

"Oh, it's cool."

"So, how often do you see your son?"

"Three to four times a year. But lately I've been able to see him more since I'm out of school now."

"How do you feel about him living so far away?

"It doesn't bother me like it used to. They live in a really nice neighborhood and she's taking good care of him, so that's what really counts."

"How long have you and she been apart?"

"She and I separated right before my son's fifth birthday."

"Can I ask why?" I'd pressed the issue.

"It wasn't anything huge. We just grew apart."

"Come on, now, be honest. You know you cheated on her."

"I'm being honest," he'd tried to convince me. He continued to tell me about his past relationship with his son's mother and then we switched gears and talked a little about my past relationship with Duke. To protect the guilty, which would be me, I refused to give him specific details pertaining to real names or the actual cities where my ex-men resided. I did, however, let the cat out the bag that Bishop had another woman and that I was the chick on the side.

At that time, Agent Sean had seemed very disappointed in me after I told him about the status of my relationship.

"I know you know that you're selling yourself short," he stated.

I didn't respond. I'd turned my head and looked out of the window.

He reached across the table and grabbed both of my hands. "Look at me," he instructed me. I'd turned my head back around to face him. "Are you happy?" he continued.

"What do you mean, like right now?"

"I'm talking about your situation with your man."

"I have my good days," I told him.

"Okay. But are you happy?"

I sat there and thought for a moment before I answered his question. It didn't take me long to weigh the pros and the cons and discover that I really had not been happy. But with everything looming over my head then, I'd had to take what I got. Bishop may have been playing me, but he was keeping a roof over my head, lining my pockets with weekly allowances, and making monthly payments on my whip.

Where else could I have gotten a nigga to pick up the tab for my living expenses? Nowhere. So I thought I might as well suck it up and deal with his bullshit before he replaced me like Duke did.

To close Agent Sean's mouth, I'd lied and told him that I was fine and I had plans to leave Bishop high and dry once I got my act together. He acted as if he believed me, but then again one could never tell. Men sure know how to put on a facade when they need to. But let me be the first to say that women have mastered it. And that's some real shit!

Once we'd finished eating, he'd offered to take me to a movie, but I declined. I had to remind myself that I was living here in New Jersey

on Bishop's tab. He had provided me with everything I needed, so I had already played myself
by accepting his first date. And to accept an extended date would be blatant disrespect to
Bishop. I knew it didn't seem like it, but I had
some morals. So, after I'd thanked him for breakfast, I gave him a warm hug. In hindsight, I
wished I would've jumped in his truck and told
him to drive far away from here. But that was
only a dream!

I woke up when I heard Jimmy's voice.
"Good morning, Mama."

"Good morning, baby. How did you sleep?"

"Oh, I slept good," he told her.

"What's for breakfast?"

"I gotta few boiled eggs in the pot on the
stove. And there's still some coffee left, so help
yourself."

"Is there enough for everyone?" he asked.

"Who cares? You just go in there and get
yourself something to eat."

"All right, Mama," he replied, and then he
walked away from her. He had to walk by me to
get to the kitchen, so as he passed me, he
stopped and kissed me on my forehead. "Good
morning, sweet pea. Did you get any sleep?"
He smiled

His slimy, wet lips sent an electric shock
through my body. Once again I felt violated to

the core. Not only did this guy almost kill me again, he forced the organs on the inside of my body to shut down. I'd urinated, and my pants were soaked. The smell coming from my pants was unbearable, and I wanted this nightmare to be over. I swear I would've rather had Bishop or the Carter brothers to torture me than to go through this shit. How much more of this was I going to have to take?

Instead of answering his stupid-ass question, I turned my focus toward the floor. I couldn't look at him, because I wanted to kill him. With the amount of anger and rage I had built up inside of me I could kill him without thinking twice.

"Oh, she's being shy, Mama," he commented playfully.

"Who cares?!" the old lady replied as she kept her attention glued to the TV.

"Are you hungry?" he continued to question me.

"No," I replied, my voice barely audible.

"You need to hose her down and put her on some clean clothes. Her body is reeking with that pee smell," his mother spoke up.

"Think that dress I took off the other girl will fit her?" he wanted to know.

"You'll never know unless you try," she told him.

At last I was going to get cleaned up. It took for me to almost die and piss on myself for this loser to do something. Damn, I wished that the tables were turned. I swear I'd make both of these people pay.

Jimmy wheeled me to the bathroom door. He untied me and carried me into the bathroom over his shoulders. I couldn't feel my legs because they were numb. But I could move my arms.

After Jimmy brought me into the bathroom, he shut the lid of the toilet stool and sat me down on it. He turned on the shower water and held his hand under the spout until he was satisfied with the temperature. "I think this is hot enough," he said.

I didn't comment on it one way or another. At this point, I was helpless. I couldn't say or do anything. I watched this fucking pervert as he stripped me down to nothing and placed me inside of their filthy-ass bathtub. And when he bathed me, I saw the different expressions he made when he washed certain parts of my body. For instance, when he washed between my legs and my breasts he smiled a little bit. I could tell that he was getting aroused. And when he started saying that he enjoyed washing me up, I knew that this would be an ongoing thing of his.

"After I wash you up, I am going to put you in this pretty dress I got saved for you," he said cheerfully.

Finally my shower time was up. He didn't bathe me the way I would've done it, but the fact that I was out of those pissy clothes made this trip to the bathroom well worth it. Before we exited the bathroom he wrapped an old towel around me. I thought he was going to put me back in the wheelchair, but he didn't. Instead he carried me to a nearby bedroom. Once inside he sat me on the edge of the bed and then he grabbed a blue dress from the closet. "This is going to look pretty on you," he said. He took the towel from my body and threw it on the bed. He didn't have any clean panties for me, so I had to go raw dog. After he put the dress on me, he stepped backward so he could get a better look at me.

"Stand up so I can see how it looks on you," he instructed me.

"I can't move my legs," I told him.

"Well, let me help you then," he said, and he helped me up from the bed.

He stood me up in front of the mirror and complimented me on how great I looked in this little-ass dress. It looked like something that came out of Walmart. Jimmy didn't think so though. He rambled on about how I needed to get my hair fixed and put on some makeup so I could look pretty for him. I was too weak to make any comments concerning this dress, my hair, or some cheap-ass makeup. I just wanted him to sit me down and never touch me again.

"Guess what I am going to do for you?" he said, all giddy.

"What?" I replied, unenthused.

"I am going to put some of Mama's lipstick on you so you can look pretty while we are eating breakfast this morning. So what'cha think about that?" he asked me.

I wanted to tell him to go to hell. But I decided against it. I couldn't handle another episode of him trying to choke the life out of me. So I just left well enough alone.

This fucking maniac put his mother's lipstick on my mouth just like he told me he would. And before we returned to the TV room he cleaned off the wheelchair and strapped me back down in it. As we approached the entryway he announced to his mother that we were coming. "Mama, you're going to be so proud when you see what I've done to Lynise."

"I don't care what you've done to her. I told you I don't like her, so leave me alone," she said.

"Ahhh, Mama, don't act like that. She's gonna be my wife. So it's important to me that you two get along." He pressed the issue.

"Oh hush, boy, she ain't no good for you. All she's gonna do is break your heart like the rest of them. Remember we just caught her in a lie less than eight hours ago."

"Mama, I know. But people can change."

"I see you're gonna have to learn the hard way," she stated. She was hell-bent on exposing me to her son. This guy has some mental issues, so this lady was able to manipulate him without any outside interferences.

I wondered what type of medicine they were taking. Because whatever it was, she had to be giving him a double dose of it. One minute Jimmy was walking around here sane and then twenty minutes later he was ready to take my fucking head off. Something just was not adding up.

"You know that when she peed on herself some of it got on the floor?"

"Yes, ma'am. I saw it."

"Well good, because I'm gonna need you to get it up before I end up slipping and falling on the floor because of it."

"I got it, Mama. I'm going to get it up after we eat breakfast."

"Is that what you're about to do? Because it looks like you are taking her out of this house with all that lipstick on her lips."

"No, Mama. I just wanted her to look pretty while we were eating."

"Is that my lipstick on her lips?" she pointed out.

"I used the one that you don't use anymore."

"You better not be lying to me, boy," she threatened.

"I'm not, Mama," Jimmy assured her as he continued to push me toward the kitchen. Immediately after we arrived in the kitchen, Jimmy pushed me up to the wobbly kitchen table. He pranced around the kitchen like he was a fucking chef. He pulled a pack of scrapple from the refrigerator and fried it, leaving the edges of it crisp and burnt. The kitchen smelled a hot mess. "Here you go, beautiful," he said as he placed the plate of boiled eggs and two slices of well-cooked scrapple in front of me. I scanned the plate for a brief moment, and I had to admit that it didn't look half bad. I figured that either I was starving or my eyes were playing tricks on me.

Jimmy sat next to me and fed me until everything on my plate was gone. "Mama, she ate everything I put on her plate," he announced.

"Who cares? I'm going to my room," she told him, and left.

Once again Jimmy and I were alone. So this would be a great time to chip away at the wall he built from anyone outside of his mother. But when I thought back to the near-death experience that happened after midnight, I convinced myself that it wouldn't be a good idea. What I decided to do was show Jimmy that I was beginning to like him as much as he liked me.

It was evident that those other victims he killed made a lot of bad choices when it pertained to him. Jimmy was looking for acceptance. And I noticed that Jimmy was also looking for love, which was something he never got from a woman. His mother had brainwashed him into believing that she was the only woman who'd ever love him. But deep down inside of his heart there was a glimmer of hope that he could prove his mother wrong.

"Thank you for breakfast. It was really good."

Jimmy smiled. "You really liked it?" he asked.

"Yes. It was good."

Jimmy continued to beam. "I'm so glad you liked it. No one ever told me that they liked my cooking but my mama."

"Well, good. Then I'll be the first." I smiled back. I swear it was hard to put on that fake smile and act like everything was good. But I had to keep reminding myself that I was in survival mode. And if I was going to get out of here alive, then I had to play their game. Getting Jimmy to turn against his mother is the first thing. And killing him would be the last and final straw.

"Have you ever had a girlfriend?" I asked him.

"One time when I was in high school. But it only lasted a few days and then she dumped me."

"Why did she dump you?"

"Because she wanted me to give her money so she could hang out with her friends. But I didn't have a lot of money to give her. Me and mama were poor. So when I couldn't give her what she wanted, she told me not to talk to her anymore and started dating this other guy in school. I used to see them hug and kiss near the girls bathroom all the time. And when I would see it, all the other guys and girls used to make fun of me and call me stupid."

"Ahh . . . really? That wasn't cool."

"I know. She broke my heart."

"What grade were you in when that happened?"

"I was a junior."

"So did you graduate from that school?"

"No. Mama took me out of that school and put me in another school."

"Did you graduate from the new school?"

"Yeah. And Mama was proud too."

I forced myself to smile. "That's good. And you should have been proud too."

"I was." He smiled bashfully.

"So how long have you been driving cabs?"

"About ten years now."

"What were you doing before you started driving cabs?"

"I worked as a janitor at the high school I graduated from. But after working there for eight years I decided to do something easier."

"Have you ever thought about having kids?"

"No. I don't think I'd be a good daddy."

"But why not?"

"Well, because sometimes I slip up and do stupid things. And babies require a lot of work."

"Well, don't beat yourself up about it, because babies are cute little things and I'm sure if you had one you'd be a good father."

Surprised by my comment he said, "Are you serious? You really think so?"

"Of course I do. And with the help of your mama, you two would be unstoppable."

Jimmy paused for a second and smiled. It almost seemed as if he were trying to look through me or read my mind.

"I knew there was something special about you."

"That's so nice of you to say," I lied. I was saying all the bullshit he wanted to hear. He was soaking it up.

"Do you have kids?" he questioned me.

"No."

"Why not?"

"Just haven't found the right guy. "

"You think I could be the right guy?"

"It's possible," I said.

"Wow! You sure know how to make a guy feel good . . ." he began to say.

"That's because you deserve it."

"Well, I guess it was meant for me to kill all those girls and get rid of their bodies, because if I hadn't I wouldn't have met you."

Shocked by his confession, I asked him how many women he killed. He thought for a moment and then he said, "Probably around twenty."

After he gave me the number of victims he slaughtered, my heart felt as if it had fallen in the pit of my stomach. Was this guy fucking serious? Had he really killed that many women? I was afraid to take this conversation any further. This nutjob was crazier than I thought. Killing women came second nature to him. And with his crazy-ass mother encouraging him, he'd probably continue to kill until someone stopped him. Hopefully that someone would be me.

He reached over and placed his left hand on my left arm. "I'm sorry. Did I spook you?" I held on to my brave face and assured him that I was fine. "Oh no. I'm cool," I lied once again.

"Well, since we're done here, let me clean up this mess before Mama sees it. And then we can take our butts back into the TV room. Who knows, maybe we can catch the rest of *Wife Swap*," he said, and got up from the table.

I watched this weirdo as he wiped down the table and cleaned our dishes. He definitely wanted a normal life, but he had no idea that he was going about it wrong.

What the hell was I going to do?

Chapter 13

Trust No One!

Knowing how Agent Rome and Agent Mann felt about this operation and the safety of Lynise threw my mind into a whirlwind. I tried to remain focused while the rest of the agents and I continued to search for Lynise. But the notion that two agents were totally running interference on my mission to find my witness made me look at them as enemies. And to know that they had no respect for me was really fucking with my ego. Men have it the hardest when we've got to hold our tongues. I was the HNIC, so why didn't they get it? And what was this secret that they didn't want Lynise to tell? Whatever it was, it would soon come out.

When I went down for breakfast, Agent Mann and Agent Rome were both drinking coffee and talking to Agent Zachary. Everyone except for Agent Rome smiled and spoke to me. After I spoke back, I looked at Rome and said, "Is there are a problem with you and me?"

"I don't think so," he replied.

"So why can't I get a good morning from you?" I questioned him.

"Because I'm not having a good morning."

"Well, I guess that answered that."

"Yeah, I guess it did."

I noticed Agent Zachary and Agent Mann looking at each other. I sensed that they felt out of place while Agent Rome and I were going back and forth. So instead of making it intensely awkward, I poured myself a cup of coffee and exited the kitchen.

I took a seat on the sofa in the TV room and started watching a little bit of the news. I turned up the TV volume so that I couldn't hear Agent Rome's voice as much. He and Agent Mann both lost all my respect. Bottom line.

As I began to get engrossed in the news, Agent Zachary joined me. She took a seat next to me. "Are you all right?" She spoke up first.

"Yeah, I'm good," I lied. But I really didn't want to talk about the fucked-up shit concerning Agents Rome and Mann. Both of them are pieces of shit, and I wanted to avoid any conversations involving them, especially after hearing them make plans to plot against me. I swear, if I hadn't had the gun and badge, I'd have whipped both of their asses and faced the consequences later.

"What happened back in the kitchen?"

"Look, Zachary, I don't feel like talking about it."

"But don't you think you need to?"

"No, I don't."

"But you're the head of this operation, so you've got to communicate with every one of us."

"Listen, I don't care what I am. If I choose not to communicate with you or anyone else in this house, then that's my prerogative. The main thing everyone in here needs to worry about is finding our witness and getting her back to safety. That's it. I will not entertain any bitching or drama from anyone. Do I make myself clear?"

"Yes. You've definitely made it clear."

"Good. Now let's talk about Mr. Malik Carter. Have the two of you started any dialog? I remember the last time you said that he wanted to take you out to lunch. Have you two talked about when or where you're going?"

"Yes. Last night before I left the club, he told me he wanted to take me to lunch today since I didn't have to work."

"What did you say?"

"I told him sure. So we're gonna hook up around one o'clock."

"Did he say where?"

"Well, he wanted to see where I live. But I

told him I wasn't ready for that. So he finally agreed to meet me at a restaurant called Kincaid's. He said it was in MacArthur Mall in downtown Norfolk."

"Okay. That sounds doable. Has anything else come up while you've been there?"

"Nothing yet. I've noticed that the club has some regulars. You know, small-time drug dealers and men who have regular jobs and want to stop by for a few drinks before they head home."

"Okay. Well, I guess you're gonna need to get dressed for your hot date," I teased her.

"Oh, stop it. You know I'm only doing this for you."

"I know. But be careful. Remember who he's related to."

"Trust me, I'm on guard. But I want to ask you, am I gonna wear a wire?"

"No. I don't see a need to. But I do want you to use your phone to record your whole conversation."

"Okay. I can do that."

"Sounds like a plan," I said, and then I patted her on her thigh. I got to my feet when Agents Mann and Rome walked into the TV room. But somehow they mistook it as my trying to avoid them. "You don't have to leave because of us," Agent Rome commented.

"Oh, no, that's not what's happening. I was about to leave anyway. Gotta go hop in the shower so I can start the day," I told him.

"Oh, okay," Rome replied.

I wasn't about to get into a pissing match with that bitch-ass nigga. So, I excused myself and made my way to the shower.

Before I hopped in the shower, I went into my bedroom to pick out a suit of clothes for today. While I was going through my things I overheard Agent Rome and Agent Mann talking to Agent Zachary about her experience at Club Diamonds. But first they asked her about her upcoming date. "Nervous?" Rome asked.

"Kind of."

"Well don't be, because we're gonna be there watching out for you," Rome assured her.

"I know you will," I heard her say.

"So, how are things at the club otherwise?" Rome probed her.

"Well, it's not as bad as I thought it would be."

"You never mentioned anything about the other girls in the club. Is there a lot of chick fighting going on?"

"Well, yeah, the strippers keep a lot of drama going. But other than that, it's just a club of naked women and hard-up men throwing money around like their minds are going bad."

"So, when that guy Malik comes around, does he normally stay in his back office, because I remember only seeing him once when Agent Mann and I were there."

"Pretty much. Oh, and now that I think about it, I saw a couple of guys going back to his office last night without being escorted by any of the bouncers, which I thought was weird. No one goes behind the stage without being escorted. So when that happened I became a little suspicious."

"Do you think they were the Carter brothers?"

"I wasn't sure."

"Did they have anything in their hands that looked like it could've been money or drugs?"

"No. They didn't have anything in their hands."

"Hmm . . . I wonder who they could've been?" I heard Rome say.

"I wanted to ask the bartender who they were, but I decided not to because I think she's Malik's watchdog. I've heard a few of the girls in there complain about how certain things go down in the club while Malik isn't there, yet he still finds out about it."

"Well, I'm glad you used good judgment. Just do what we tell you to do and we'll handle the rest. And hopefully your boss upstairs won't have you working this detail too much longer," I heard Rome tell Zachary.

"Hopefully you're right," Zachary replied. I could tell that her heart really wasn't in this. She sounded a bit overwhelmed to say the least. And having Agents Rome and Mann in her fucking ears with a bunch of negative chatter wasn't helping the situation.

I saw through all of that bullshit. Too bad Zachary didn't. I see that I might be on my own with this operation. That is, if Agent

Humphreys decides to side with them. If that happens, then I'm going to be up a river without a paddle.

When I thought I had heard enough of everyone's bullshit, I headed to the shower. Bathing in some hot water might be the therapy I needed. Who knows, I may even get courageous enough to pistol-whip Agent Rome and Agent Mann and send them back to New Jersey in a UPS box.

It wasn't like they wouldn't deserve it.

Chapter 14

Hatching Out a Plan

Day five rolled in slowly while I was still strapped down to the fucking wheelchair. I had to face the music that these accommodations were fucked up to the tenth power. I was sitting in a fucking wheelchair. I couldn't feel my legs for nothing in the world. I actually couldn't feel anything below my waist. The only freedom they gave me was to be able to talk freely without the old rag they had once tied around my mouth. Sorry to say that all ended when someone knocked on the front door. My heart rate picked up rapidly. *KNOCK, KNOCK, KNOCK.*

Jimmy was asleep, but after he heard someone knocking on the front door he jumped to his feet. His face looked panic-stricken. "Mama, are you expecting someone?" he whispered. His mama was sitting on the love seat a few feet away from me, watching TV.

"No. I don't know who that could be."

I watched them closely while they were trying to figure things out. While Jimmy was trying to figure out who was at his front door, his mama turned her sights on me. "Before we do anything, we need to tie her mouth back up in case she tries to scream," his mama said.

My heart continued to race, but I held my composure. It was important to convince them that I wouldn't open my mouth. Having my mouth untied would give me a fair advantage to let someone know that I was being held captive. Who knows, it could be the police standing outside the front door. If it was, there was no doubt in my mind that they were coming for me. "You don't have to tie up my mouth. I promise I won't say a word," I whispered. Unfortunately my words meant nothing. Jimmy's mother wrapped that gag around my mouth quicker than I could blink. Immediately after, she instructed Jimmy to watch me while she found out who was at the front door.

By this time, anxiety engulfed my entire body. *Please, please, please, let it be somebody who'll save me,* I thought to myself. *Lord, I know I have done some bad things but if you get me out of this jam, I will change my life from this day forward,* my thoughts continued. I literally said a small prayer. I just hoped that God heard me.

The person at the door knocked a few more times before Jimmy's mama answered it. "Who is it?" I heard her ask.

"It's the mailman, ma'am. I have a package that I need you to sign for," he stated.

"I didn't send for a package," she told him.

"Is your name Mrs. Francis Beckford?" I heard the man yell.

"Yes, it is. But I still don't know of any package that's supposed to come here, so can you just leave it on the porch?"

"No, ma'am. I have to get you to sign for it." He pressed the issue.

"Well, I'm not in the mood to sign anything right now, so just send it back to where it came from," she replied.

"Okay, ma'am. As you wish," he said, and then all communication ceased.

When the crazy old lady walked back to the TV room, she looked suspiciously at me. But then she turned her attention to Jimmy. "Do you think that mailman really had something for us?" she asked him.

Jimmy looked puzzled. "If he did, I don't know who it could've came from."

"And neither do I," she said as she sat back down. She got back into her TV show with no problems. Jimmy acted a little paranoid for about an hour or so. But then he calmed himself down and retreated to doing his own thing.

I sat there feeling sorry for myself. I mean,

how in the hell could I have gotten so close to getting someone to help me get out of here? The fucking mailman was right there at their front door. He was right there and now he's gone. What kind of justice am I going to get for myself? It's a crying shame that I have no damn family who'd put out a missing person's report on me. It felt really fucked up to be living in a world and no one really gave a damn about you except for a fucking retard. This guy basically said that we were soul mates. Now, how fucked up in the head is he? He and I've never dated. And so far we haven't had sex, so why is it that he cared more about me than the motherfuckers I grew up with or known all my life? Was I that fucked up as a person that nobody liked me? Okay, granted, I've done some messed-up shit in my life, but I didn't deserve this type of treatment. One minute he and his mama are putting their hands on me, and then the next minute this goofball is telling me that he loves me. Is this how life will end for me? If so, then kill me now.

"Mama, I'm off to work," Jimmy announced. Since I'd been there Jimmy and his mother took shifts to watch me. He'd sit in the TV room with me during the day and she'd watch me at night. It was eleven-thirty P.M., so his shift with the cab company was about to begin.

"I'm gonna need you to pick up a few things

from the store, so take this list and stop by there on your way home," she told him.

He took the list from her hands and stuffed it in his front shirt pocket. "Be good for Mama," he said, looking at me.

"She'd better if she knows what's good for her," his mother commented.

Now, of course I wasn't feeling her smart-ass remark, but what was I supposed to do about it? I couldn't curse her ass out. And I couldn't beat her ass, so I just chalked it up and reminded myself that I'd have my way with her one of these damn days.

Jimmy eventually made his way out the front door. His mother sat in her usual spot and turned the TV channel to the news. Under normal circumstances I hated to watch the news channels. I had no interest in the local news. But I'd become obsessed. While the old lady kept up with the weather and the local news, I was doing the same thing, minus the weather.

The old lady and I heard about the big layoff at the Portsmouth Shipyard and the increase in tolls, and then a segment about the serial killing came on. My heart skipped a beat when the reporter stated that the homicide detectives had been getting a lot of tips but no arrests had been made. Hearing that news, I felt a load of shit starting to weigh down on my shoulders.

"Tonight Newport News police are still looking for two women who went missing a few weeks ago and the person or persons responsible for it. They said they have some strong leads. One of those leads involved a witness who said they last saw one of those women get into a taxi cab. Now while that may be a good tip, the police are still asking anyone who has more information on these women or their whereabouts to please contact the tip line at 1-888-LOCKUUP."

After the reporter ended the broadcast, the old lady got up from her seat. "I don't want to hear a peep out of you," she said, and then she left the TV room. She returned a couple minutes later with a cell phone. Immediately after she sat back down she got Jimmy on the line. "Hey, son, I think we got a problem," she said.

"What's going on?" I heard him ask. The volume on her phone was up really high. The only reason for that would be because she needed a hearing aid.

"I just saw the news. And they're reporting that they got a witness saying that they saw one of those girls get into a cab."

"Did they give the name of the cab? Or say what color it was?" he wanted to know.

"The news reporter didn't mention that."

"Well, good. Then I guess we have nothing to worry about."

"Look, son, I just want you to be careful. You never know who's out there watching."

"Mama, I'm a big boy. I can handle anything that comes my way," I heard him say.

"Okay. Well, call me in a couple of hours just so I know that you're all right."

"Sure, I can do that."

"I love you."

"I love you too."

After the old lady disconnected the call, she sat the phone by her side and continued to watch TV. I went back to watching TV as well. But I couldn't stop thinking about how she was telling him to be careful. She acted as if he was the one in harm's way. Was she fucking smoking crack or something? I mean, really, lady!

Please wake up and smell the fucking coffee.

In addition to the drama surrounding this lady warning Jimmy to be careful, I also couldn't shake the fact that there was a witness who saw one of those girls get into a cab. I was left to wonder about whether this information would eventually lead back to Jimmy's psychotic ass. Would they put two and two together and bust his ass? I needed a huge miracle. This guy needed a jail cell with two beds for himself and his mother.

I mean, I was there. The cops locked my ass up for something I didn't even do. Murder was what I was charged with. And I'd had to sit behind bars until they dropped the charges and let me go. And these maniacs broke every law under the sun. First one was kidnapping, holding someone against their will, assault, among other things. But yes, these monsters needed

128

to be locked underneath a fucking jail. I realized they weren't sick, they were fucking criminals. They were sick, fucking criminals. I swore, when and if I were finally ever freed, I would kill the bastards with my own hands if given the chance. I wanted to kill the motherfuckers slow too. I wanted them to feel every ounce of paid I felt.

They deserved it.

Chapter 15

Having Cocktails

I sat at the bar of the restaurant Kincaid's when Agent Zachary and Malik walked in. She was all smiles and so was Malik. Seeing this guy Malik for the first time in broad daylight was quite surprising. Mr. Carter stood at a modest height for a man. His build was quite impressive. I could tell that he worked out. But what caught my eye was his jewelry collection. In my mind a strip club owner, and especially one who's related to a couple of notorious gangsters, would wear a lot of flashy jewelry. The guys in the rap videos wore some expensive diamond jewelry, so I imagined that a black club owner would mimic their behavior. Sorry to say I was wrong. Malik had on a gold Rolex President watch and one diamond-and-gold pinky ring. It was nothing extravagant. But everyone who saw him knew he lived well.

The restaurant's host escorted them to their table. I watched him while he watched Agent Zachary's ass switch from side to side. There was no doubt what he had on his mind. After the host handed them menus he left them alone to decide.

Soon a waiter greeted them and took their drink orders. When he returned he had a glass of Chardonnay and a couple shots of Grand Marnier in a wineglass. Halfway through their cocktails the waiter brought their meals. I noticed that Agent Zachary had shrimp tossed in pasta while Malik had a grilled chicken breast with some brown sauce poured over it and a side of yellow rice. Both of their meals looked great.

While they were eating away, Malik got a call on his cell phone. He excused himself from the table and walked out of the restaurant and into the mall. The moment he went out of sight, I looked back at Agent Zachary. She returned the look and hunched her shoulders to say she didn't know what was going on. She and I sat in our seats and waited patiently for his return.

One minute passed. Then two minutes passed. And then five minutes passed. And there was still no Malik. I was very curious to see what was taking him so fucking long to get back to the table with Agent Zachary. I paid the bartender for my tab and then I slid off the barstool. As soon as I exited the restaurant I saw Malik take a small plastic bag from a guy who looked to be every bit of nineteen years old, if not younger. I wanted desperately to know what was in the bag, but I wasn't there to build a drug case against Malik. I was only interested in getting information that could possibly help me find Lynise. Everything else was secondary.

Malik passed me on his way back into the restaurant. I, on the other hand, was interested in seeing where that young guy was going. I ended up following him to the parking garage, where a late model, white Range Rover with dark tinted windows was waiting for him.

Everything happened so fast. As soon as he got inside the truck it pulled off into the sunset. I wasn't close enough to the truck to see the driver. I was so close, yet so far away.

Luckily, I was able to rebound by taking a couple of screenshots of the license plate with my cell phone while the truck was pulling out. I planned to check on the plate when I got back to the safe house. I was hoping I would get a good hit.

I got into my car and sat there for a moment trying to figure out what I was going to do next. I couldn't leave the mall, because Agent Zachary was still having lunch with that Malik guy. I also knew that I couldn't go back into the restaurant for fear that I'd stick out like a sore thumb. Malik would spot me immediately.

After careful thinking, I decided to stay in my car and wait for Agent Zachary and Malik to leave so I could follow her back to the safe house. It was imperative that I kept a close watch on Agent Zachary. After hearing Agents Mann and Rome talk shit about me to Agent Zachary, I felt it was my duty to make her feel as little stress as possible. I figured that she might be my ticket to finding Lynise. And if she wasn't, then I'd have to move forward with another plan. Either way, I had to protect her.

It seemed like it was taking forever for Agent Zachary to end her date with Malik. I was becoming impatient because I wanted to get back to the safe house so I could log into the DMV database and find out who registered the license plate on the white Range Rover. I became so anxious that I called Agent Humphreys.

"I need you to look up a plate for me," I started off saying.

"What's the state?"

"Virginia."

"What's the plate number?"

"Echo-Bravo-Oscar-2891," I said.

"Okay. Give me a minute," he replied, and then he fell silent. "Was that plate on a 2012 white Range Rover?" Humphreys asked.

"Yes," I told him.

Five seconds later, he said, "You are not going to believe this."

"Tell me," I said anxiously.

"This vehicle is registered to Terrence Carter."

"Get the fuck out of here!" I replied with excitement.

"I am serious as a heart attack," Humphreys commented.

"What city is the vehicle registered in?"

"Virginia Beach."

"What's the address?"

"5391 Pleasure House Road."

I grabbed a pen from the cup holder in the car and wrote down the address. Before the day ended, I was going by this address to see if I could finally put a face with the last name Carter. I was ready to see who wanted Lynise dead.

Agent Zachary finally ended her lunch date with Malik. He walked her to her car, which was on the first floor of the parking garage. I was parked on the opposite side of the garage, but I was still able to see the car. Seconds after Malik kissed Agent Zachary on the cheek, he opened her car door and closed it after she sat down in the driver's seat. He said a few words to her as she drove her car in reverse. And when she put the car in drive he watched her until she drove away.

To avoid bringing heat to Agent Zachary or me, I exited the parking garage on the side where I was parked. And as soon as I paid the toll clerk, I dialed Agent Zachary's cell phone number and raced toward Monticello Avenue. She answered on the first ring. "Hello?"

"Are you okay?" I asked her.

"Yes, I'm fine. I'm just glad that it's finally over."

"What took you so long?"

"I couldn't stop him from touching my hands and talking me to death."

"Did he mention anything about why it took him so long to get back into the restaurant?"

"All he did was apologize and say that he had to meet with someone in the mall."

"Well, yeah, he met some young thug. And I caught the thug handing him a plastic bag. I couldn't tell what was in it. But right after Malik took the bag, he and the guy parted ways."

"Did you see where the guy went?"

"Yeah, I followed him into the parking garage and saw him get into a white Range Rover. I got Agent Humphreys to run the license plate number and come to find out that the vehicle is registered to a Terrence Carter."

"You're kidding, right?!"

"No, I am not. And I've got a physical address to prove it."

"So, what are you gonna do with it?"

"I'm gonna go by there and see if I can put a face to the name."

"You're not going over there alone, are you?"

"No. You're going with me," I replied nonchalantly.

"Do you think that this is a good idea?"

"Sure I do. Now tell me where you are so we can meet up."

"I just merged onto Highway 264."

"Okay. Drive slowly, because I'm coming that way too."

"How can I drive slow on the highway?"

"Well, do the speed limit and stay in the far right lane until I catch up to you," I instructed her.

"Why don't I get off the next exit and wait for you?"

"All right. Do that and I'll see you in about five minutes."

"Okeydokey," she said.

Finding Agent Zachary was fairly easy. She was in parking lot of a Hardee's restaurant awaiting my arrival. I pulled up next to her rented vehicle and rolled down the driver's side window. I smiled at her.

"Why are you so happy?" she asked.

"It feels like I just won the freaking lottery or something."

"Well, what's the game plan, Mr. Lottery Winner?"

"I was thinking it would be a good idea if you left your rental car here and climbed in the car with me. But then I figured it wouldn't make sense to drive all the way back down here after we left Virginia Beach. So why don't you follow me and when we get close to the house, I'll give you further instructions from there."

"Okay. Cool. Let's do that," she agreed.

I keyed the home address of Terrence Carter into my GPS, and a couple of seconds later the directions popped on the screen. As I drove out of the Hardee's parking lot Agent Zachary followed. It took us approximately twenty minutes to drive from Norfolk to the Virginia Beach address.

The neighborhood was called Mason Brick Estates, and it was beautiful hands down. The homes had to be in the ballpark of one million and up. The only amenity missing was that the community wasn't gated.

I pulled over to the side of the street and motioned for Agent Zachary to pull her car beside mine. "What's up?" she said after she rolled down her window.

"The house is located on Pleasure House Road. According to my GPS, go two blocks up and then make a right. After you make a right, drive slowly and tell me if the white Range Rover is parked outside."

"What if someone's outside?"

"Just act normal and look like you're lost. As a matter of fact, call me now so I can talk you through it," I said calmly. I needed her to know that I was in this thing with her.

She took a deep breath and then she exhaled. "Here goes nothing," she said as she began to drive away.

"Call me now," I yelled.

"I'm doing it now," she yelled back.

One second later my cell phone rang. "Are you up here?" she asked.

"Yes, I'm up here."

"Okay, well, I'm putting you on speaker right now."

"All right. But keep your phone low so no one sees it."

"Foster, I know. Please be quiet, because you're making me nervous."

"Okay. I won't say anything else. But you've got to communicate with me as soon as you get close to the house."

"Okay. I'm making the right turn now," she said. "What's the house number?"

"It's 5391."

"Oh . . . okay," she said, and then she went silent. "Foster, I see it," she blurted out. I could tell by her voice that her heart rate picked up.

"Do you see the white Range Rover?"

"Yes. It's in the driveway. And it's parked next to a black Aston Martin."

"What color is the house? How big is it?" I pressed her with more questions.

"It's a brick house, dark mahogany color. It's two stories and it is massive."

"What kind of window treatments do they have? Can you see inside the house from your car?"

"Oh shit! Somebody is coming out of the house."

"Who is it?"

"If this Terrence Carter guy is brown skinned and tall, then I see our guy. Shit! He's looking directly at me," she replied, her voice cracking.

"Agent Zachary . . . calm down! What is the matter with you? You aren't acting like an undercover agent right now," I snapped.

"I know. I know. It's just that I don't want to blow my cover," she whispered as if someone would hear her.

"Listen, just act like you're looking for someone's house. You know, stop the car at the house two doors down from his house and then drive away. And if you want to do it again, drive a little ways up the block and stop in front of another house and then drive off again."

"Okay, that's what I'll do," she said, a little more confident.

"While you're doing that, can you still see him?"

"No. I think he might've gotten into one of the cars."

"And where are you?"

"I'm three houses away from his."

"Look in the rearview mirror and tell me if you can see him now."

"No. I don't see him."

"Well, slow down at the next house you come to and see if you can see his house from there."

"Oh shit! There he goes. I see him coming down the street behind me."

"All right, Agent Zachary. Calm down. Don't

move. Keep your foot on the brake and act as if you're looking at the house."

"Okay," I heard her say, and then she sighed heavily.

"Where is he? Has he passed you yet?"

"He's coming now," she replied, sounding a bit alarmed.

"Remember what I said. Be calm. . . ." I began to coach her, but then she cut me off.

"No, I'm looking for 5406 Pleasure House Road. I'm beginning to think that I have the wrong address," I heard her say.

"You're absolutely right, because there is no 5406 Pleasure House Road. You may want to call the person you're looking for and tell them you're lost," I heard a male's voice say, even though it was faint.

"I'm gonna do just that," Agent Zachary replied.

"Good luck," I heard the guy say.

"Thank you," Agent Zachary said.

I waited a few minutes before I spoke. I wanted to make sure the coast was clear. Thankfully Agent Zachary spoke first. "He's gone."

"Which way is he going?" I asked her.

"He's making a left on the next street, so he's coming back your way."

"Has he turned the corner yet?"

"He's doing it now, so you may wanna duck down."

"I'm on it as we speak," I told her. Instead of scrunching down in my seat I leaned the driver's side seat back. This helped me to still be able to see Mr. Carter as he drove by my car.

Like clockwork Mr. Carter came rolling in my direction. My windows were semitinted, so I had another way of being obscured from anyone outside the car. After he passed, I spoke into the receiver of my cell phone. "He just rolled by."

"What do we do now?" Agent Zachary asked me.

"We're gonna go back to the safe house."

"Roger that."

Chapter 16

The Following Night

Despite the warning that Jimmy's mother gave him the night before after seeing the news segment, Jimmy acted like he was untouchable. He bragged about getting away with all the lives he had taken. This guy was a fucking monster. I mean, unprecedented.

Jimmy came into the TV room after he got ready for work. He had three hours to hang around the house until his shift started. I was in my usual spot, strapped down to the wheelchair only a few feet away from the TV. "Mama, how do I look? Think I can pick up another hot date tonight?" he asked. He twirled in the middle of the floor like he was a fucking Calvin Klein model. He looked a fucking mess, displaying an old button-down shirt, a pair of khaki pants, and a busted pair of loafers.

His mother was sitting in her favorite chair watching TV. "What hot date? I thought you said she was the one?" she replied nonchalantly after she took her eyes off the TV screen and looked him over from head to toe.

"She is, Mama. But I just don't want to put all my eggs in one basket in case she screws me over."

"I'm glad you're finally talking with some sense. But I don't think it's a good idea for you to go out there and mess with any more of those girls. I told you last night that the reporter said that those cops got some tips that came into their office. So don't go out there and do something stupid. Leave those girls alone for right now. Let the cops think that you aren't out there roaming their streets anymore. And then they'll forget all about you."

"Mama, I was just kidding. I'm not messing around with none of those girls tonight."

"Thank goodness."

Jimmy walked over to me and kissed me on my forehead. "I was just teasing a few minutes ago, so don't pay any attention to what I said. You are my one and only love. And as soon as the time is right, I'm gonna give you the ring my daddy gave to my mama and then we're gonna get married." I wanted to vomit in my fucking mouth. His wet kisses were the worst thing ever. His lips felt like an old mildewy washcloth.

"Oh, leave her alone, will you?!" she spat.

"But I'm in love, Mama. I've never loved a woman like I love her."

"Boy, you don't know what love is."

"Yes, I do."

"Then tell me," she instructed him.

"Love is when you can't do without someone. And that's how I feel about her," he explained.

"Well, you go ahead and continue to act like you're in love and I'm gonna go in my bedroom so I can get some peace and quiet," she told him, and then she got to her feet.

Immediately after she took her first step she slipped and fell to the floor. "Awwwwwww!" she screamed.

Jimmy rushed to her side. "Oh my God, Mama, are you all right?"

"I think I broke my hip," she said. I could tell that she was in pure agony as she laid on her right side.

Very concerned, Jimmy said, "Come on, Mama, let me help you get off the floor."

"Awwwwwww!" she screamed louder while Jimmy tried to pull her up from underneath both of her arms. "It's not going to work, so just leave me lying here," she told him.

"No, I won't do that. I'm gonna use all of my strength to lift you up," he told her.

"No, son, it's not gonna work. You're gonna

have to call a paramedic," she managed to say while she cried out to Jimmy.

"Oh no, Mama, you know we can't let nobody in here. Remember, we got Lynise sitting right there."

"Well, why don't you think of a better way to get me off the floor?"

"Mama, you're gonna have to trust me. So when I say lift I want you to press your weight against me."

"But it's not gonna work, son."

"Yes it is, Mama. You got to trust me," he said in a coaching manner.

I sat there and smiled. I can honestly say that I was enjoying seeing Jimmy's mother in all that pain. I was enjoying it so much, his mother saw me smiling and she nearly spit fire at my ass.

"Jimmy, look at her. She's laughing in our faces," she pointed out while she cried. She was seething, so furious with me that I could almost see smoke coming from her ears.

Jimmy wasn't too happy to see a smirk on my face either. But at that point, I could not care less how they saw me. I was the fucking victim, not her. Shit! If he had left me where I was, then I wouldn't be here to start with, much less be in her face and laughing at her old miserable ass!

Jimmy stood up. He got in my face, his words coming out in a hail of spit. "You think that this is funny?"

"No," I lied. But he didn't buy it.

And that's when he pulled back and hurled a backhanded slap against my face. It seemed like my entire left jaw had cracked. Pain crippled me that instant. I screamed at the top of my voice, "Fuck you and your mama! I am so tired of y'all! I hope the bitch never walks again!" I roared.

But that outburst didn't help me at all. Before I even realized it, Jimmy had hurled more blows to my face. He knocked me into oblivion. "You think you can talk about my mama and I don't do anything about it? Bitch, are you crazy? I love my mama! And you think I'm gonna let you sit here and disrespect her?" he snapped.

Jimmy hit me so many times, I completely lost track. I felt my face get numb. And his words became one big blur. And there was nothing I could do about it.

I did, however, hear when Jimmy's mother begged him to stop hitting me. I believed that if she hadn't said a word, he would've beat me until I was a dead. Lucky me!

"Son, look at your hands." I heard his mother say.

"I know, Mama. I know."

"You gotta go and wash them off," she instructed him while she continued to cry.

I had no idea if she was crying because she felt bad for me, or if she was still in a lot of pain. I swear, I didn't know what to think anymore.

Jimmy had beat me pretty bad. I knew he had blackened both of my eyes, because I could barely see out of them. I was able to see him walk in the direction of the kitchen. Seconds later, I heard the faucet water running, so I knew he was trying to wash the blood off. And there I sat, helplessly.

A few moments later, Jimmy returned from the kitchen. He walked into the room drying his hands with a handful of paper towels.

"Jimmy, you're gonna have to come out of that bloody shirt too."

"Never mind that. I'm more concerned with getting you off the floor."

"Will you please take off that shirt? It's making me nauseous just looking at it."

"Fine, mother." He ripped the shirt off his back, threw the shirt down to the floor, and took another shot at picking her up. Doing it without causing her severe pain was not an option. She cried with every pull and tug.

"Jimmy, this is not going to work." She cried harder.

"But it has to, Mama." He was persistent.

"Honey, I know you don't want to hear this, but you're gonna have to call the paramedics."

"Listen, baby, this is what we can do," she started off saying. "You can put the gag back around her mouth and put her in the laundry room. And then when you're done, you can come in here and clean all that blood off the floor and change into another pair of pants and a shirt. And those paramedics ain't gonna know the difference," she concluded.

Jimmy stood there for a minute, thinking about what his deranged-ass mother had said. She must've convinced him that he could pull off the ultimate scam, because he grabbed the handles of my wheelchair and began to roll my ass out of the TV room.

The laundry room was dark and had a damp smell. It wasn't unbearable, but it stood out. Keep in mind I couldn't see a thing. But the drops of blood dripping from my face down to my chest made me painfully aware of what had just happened to me. At that very moment, I just wanted to die. It seemed as if I'd been running for my life as long as I could remember. And this day I could honestly say that I was tired. I was tired of living and breathing. And I wouldn't fight anymore. At least that way I could finally get some rest and think back on some good times I'd had in my life. I needed to think about something positive or else I was going to die inside.

I recalled that I had been treated good in my life at least a few times. Duke took care of me in the beginning. He used to lavish me with nice clothes, shoes, and money, and when he gave me the keys to that BMW that was the ultimate gift. I had never had a man to give me a car before. Much less a fucking luxury car. So when I got behind the wheel of it, I felt like a superstar. I felt loved. But then that all came crashing down once I found out what kind of a man Duke really was. I'd never forget when I walked into the condo he allowed me to stay in and I'd overhead him talking to his friend Dr. Gavin. When I'd heard them talking about photos they had of young pregnant girls and that they were taking their newborn babies, I'd almost shit in my pants. I couldn't believe my ears. I'd thought Duke was different. I'd thought he was a legitimate businessman. But he wasn't. Duke was into some black market baby-snatching type of illegal adoption shit. He had actually hired a fucking doctor to snatch young girls' babies. And everything that he did has had an effect on where I was right then. Sitting in this fucking raggedy-ass house with these two deranged-ass people. Will this shit ever end? What would happen to me if I were ever able to get out of this fucking smelly-ass house? Would I find myself in something else life threatening? It just seemed like I couldn't ever get a fucking break.

While I sat there with the desire to just wither away, I heard a lot of rumbling around in the other room.

"Did you call them yet?" I heard his mother ask.

"Mama, let me get the rest of this blood off the floor and I will call them."

"But I don't know how much longer I can lie on the floor like this."

"Okay, Mama. I'm gonna call them now."

A minute or so passed and I heard Jimmy speaking with a 9-1-1 operator. He put the call on speaker so the operator could hear his mother speak. "My mama fell on the floor and she thinks she broke her hip."

"How do you know she broke her hip?" the woman asked.

"She's right here, so I'm gonna let you talk to her."

"Ma'am, are you on the phone?" the operator asked.

"Yes, I'm here."

"What's your name, ma'am?"

"My name is Mrs. Francis Beckford."

"All right, Mrs. Beckford, can you tell me what happened?"

"Yes. I got up from the chair in my TV room and when I tried to step away, I tripped and fell down on my hip. And it hurts so bad, so that's why I think I broke it."

"What is your address?" The woman kept questioning Jimmy's mother.

"I'm at 842 Ocean View Avenue."

"Okay. Just stay where you are and I will have a paramedic to you in a few minutes."

"I will, thank you," Mrs. Beckford replied.

After Jimmy's mother hung up the phone she instructed him to get her purse from her bedroom. I heard Jimmy scurry down the hallway.

A few moments later, he scurried back down the hallway and into the room. "Here, Mama, I got your purse."

"Just put it on the chair so I won't forget it when the paramedics take me out of here."

"Okay, Mama, I'm setting it right here," I heard him say.

Once again, I couldn't see anything but I heard the loud sirens blaring from the paramedics. I even heard sirens blaring from a fire truck. And for the first time, a small tab of hope came over me. Was I finally about to be rescued? Was this my chance to live and breathe again? Or was I fooling myself? Whenever it happens, I wouldn't be able to control it.

I started hearing at least three sets of footsteps. And then voices came immediately after. "Where is she?" the first male voice asked.

"She's in the TV room," Jimmy replied.

"Yes, I'm back here," she yelled.

"From one to ten, and ten being the worst, how bad is the pain?" the same male voice asked.

"It's an eight," she told him.

"Can you move?" another voice asked.

"No. My son tried to pick me up a few times, but it didn't work. My hip was hurting too bad.

So I told him to leave me alone and call you guys."

"Okay. Well, we're gonna all lift you up at the same time and put you on this gurney. Now, keep in mind this is going to hurt, but the quicker we get you to the hospital, the faster we can get you feeling better."

"I don't care. I just want to get this pain to stop."

"Ma'am, we will take care of you. Now, when we count to three we're gonna all lift you up, so take a deep breath."

"Okay," I heard her say, but it was more like a soft cry.

Without another moment's notice the men counted loudly, and when they got to the number three I heard an agonizing scream and I knew they had lifted her into the air and laid her down on the gurney. Her cries became more and more intense. She made sure they knew that she was in a lot of pain.

"Okay, the hard part is over. Now we're going to get you to the hospital," one man said.

"Is she allergic to anything?" another man asked.

"No. She's not allergic to anything," Jimmy replied.

"Sounds great. Are you going to follow us to the hospital?" one of the familiar voices asked.

"Yes. I'm going to get some of her things and I will be right behind you," Jimmy said. They didn't know it, but he was trying to rush them out of the house. And I knew that if that happened, God knows when I'd have another chance at getting out of there.

"Okay, well, I'm gonna help Jason put this nice lady into the ambulance. And then Chuck and I are going to head back to the fire station," one of the men said.

"All right, thanks, Nick."

"Don't mention it," Nick said, and then I heard footsteps leaving the house.

I felt the pressure mounting on my shoulders, because it sounded like there was only one man left in the house. So the first thought that popped in my head was to make some noise, some kind of way. But how was I going to do that when I couldn't see what was around me? It was pitch black. So the second thought popped in my head, telling me to try to make some noise with my mouth. Now, I knew it would be somewhat impossible since my mouth had been tied up, but hey, I wouldn't know if it would work if I didn't try it. *Here goes nothing,* I said to myself.

"Help . . . Help . . . Help . . . Help," I screamed, even though my words were muffled. But no one heard me, because after I stopped I heard one of the paramedics still carrying on a conversation with Jimmy.

Next I used the weight of my body to rock the wheelchair, and while I was rocking the wheelchair I began to scream again.

I rocked the wheelchair so hard that I managed to fall sideways onto the floor. *Boom!*

It felt like the whole laundry room shook. Thankfully, the loud noise from my fall got the attention of the paramedic.

"Did you hear that?" I heard the man ask.

"Yeah. That was probably my cat knocking over something in the laundry room," Jimmy lied.

"No . . . No . . . He's lying!" I screamed once more. But again my words were muffled. So I started kicking. And what do you know, my feet struck the washing machine. It was like music to my ears.

"Wait a minute, sir, that's not a cat back there. Are you hiding something?" the man asked.

"No, sir. That's my cat."

"Don't lie to me, sir. Now tell me if you've got somebody back there," the man demanded.

While he was demanding that Jimmy give him a truthful answer, I continued to kick the washing machine. I was not about to let this man get out of this house without saving me.

Suddenly I heard footsteps walking in my direction. I wanted to be optimistic, but I couldn't. Nothing in my life ever went the way I wanted it to. I was plagued with bad karma. So why would it be different this time?

"Don't go back there," I heard Jimmy warn the paramedic.

So I kept striking my feet against the washing machine.

"I'm warning you. I told you not to go back there," Jimmy said again.

But the guy kept walking to where I was.

My heart was racing uncontrollably. I finally felt as if there was a light at the end of the tunnel. And what do you know, I finally saw that light. My eyes nearly popped out of my head when the door to the laundry room opened. The light from the hallway illuminated as the white guy stood before me. He was more shocked than I was. "What the fuck is going on? Why do you have her tied up? And why is she so fucking bloody?" His questions came one after the other.

I started crying all over again. But there was no way you could see my tears from all of the blood painted on my face. "Please help me!" I begged, even though he couldn't understand what I was saying with that fucking gag. But as it turned out, he needed the help. When he reached down to take the gag from my mouth, Jimmy walked up behind the paramedic, aimed a gun at his head, and blew him into pieces. This man's entire skull exploded like it was a fucking pumpkin. All the human tissue connected to his brains splattered on me and on everything in the laundry room. I started kicking and screaming after the paramedic's dead body fell on top of me. "See what you made me do?" Jimmy screamed, and kicked me.

"Aggh!" I shrieked. Instinctively, I tried to curl into a fetal position in an attempt to stop his blows from landing in my face. His boot slammed into my abdomen, then with the force of a wrecking ball, he landed a kick to my rib cage.

"My mama was right. You ain't no different from the rest of those girls."

"What's going on? Did I hear a gunshot?" I heard the other paramedic yell as he rushed down the hall toward us. Jimmy immediately turned around and aimed his gun at the other paramedic. He pulled the trigger again and again until he ran out of bullets.

After the gunshots stopped, I heard the front door slam shut. "Oh fuck! He got away." Jimmy panicked. "Shit! What am I going to do?" he screamed as he punched the wall in the hallway. But then something popped in his head, because right after he punched the wall, he took off and ran down the hallway. "Fuck! He just drove off with Mama!" Jimmy roared. I heard the vengeance in his tone. So I knew he was about to unleash the beast inside of him.

I heard him slam the front door shut and then I heard him as he stormed back down the hallway. When he reappeared in the doorway of the laundry room, he looked down at me. "This is all your fault. You sneaky bitch! I should've raped and killed you when I let you get in my cab. But no, I had to be good and bring you home to my mama so we could all be a family. Yeah, you screwed me over. So I'm going to pay you back real good after I get us out of here."

Once Jimmy figured out that he didn't have much time to get out of here, he lifted the dead paramedic's body off me and then he wheeled me out of the laundry room. I was still covered in blood and lacerations, but Jimmy wasn't concerned about that. He was focused on getting out of there before the other paramedic called the police to the house. I had no idea how he was going to execute his escape. But I was fully aware that he had no intentions of leaving me behind. "If you take me with you, I'm only gonna slow you down." I got up the courage to say.

"Shut the fuck up before I kill you right now!" he screamed.

Chapter 17

I Can't Blow My Cover

Iarrived to the strip club about thirty minutes before Agent Zachary was scheduled to come in. I sat in the far right corner of the club, bought a beer, and began to watch the show that this black stripper was putting on.

Unconsciously, I looked down at my watch at least seven times within the first fifteen minutes that I was there. I was on edge still wondering where the hell Lynise was. And how come I and the other agents hadn't been able to find her? Had her life already been taken? I hadn't told the other agents, but I was slowly losing hope in finding her alive.

While I sipped on my beer, I noticed a couple of guys on the other side of the club swapping money for drugs. From where I sat, it looked like it was only an ounce or two of marijuana. After the buyer smelled the product, he stuffed it inside his jacket and made a toast with the guy that he gave the money to.

After that exchange I witnessed a couple of the strippers giving a couple of the guys lap dances. The rap music was booming from the deejay booth. The girls loved it.

I rocked my head to the beat and continued to sip on my beer when this very beautiful woman approached me. She looked like a twin to Evelyn Lozada from *Basketball Wives*. She had Evelyn's body and all. She gave me a huge smile.

"Can I give you a lap dance?"

"What's your name?"

"Hollywood," she said seductively, biting on the tip of her finger.

"Well, Hollywood, as much as I want to be in your company, right now isn't a good time," I told her.

"Why not? You look lonely over here all by yourself. Don't you want some company?"

"Listen, baby girl, you are as beautiful as they come. But I'm not in the mood for a lap dance right now," I explained to her.

"Are you depressed or something? Because if you are, I can take your mind off of it." She pressed the issue.

I smiled at her because she was becoming relentless. She was definitely a hustler. And if my circumstances dealing with Lynise were different I would've loved for this chick to ride my dick. "Hey, look, sunshine, I've got a lot on my mind, and all I want to do is sit here and relax. Now, if for some reason I start feeling better, then I'll call you back over here."

"Okay. Cool," she said, then she walked away.

I watched as she made her way back across the floor, and I had to admit that she was sexy as hell. That chick had a body out of this fucking world. And to see her strutting that fat ass she had started getting my dick hard, which was why I declined her offer. Having her grind on me would've fucked my head up and I would not have been focused when Agent Zachary clocked in. I needed to be on guard at all times.

Once I had guzzled down my beer, I got the waitress to give me another one. I had to act like I was a bona fide patron and not an undercover agent. So after the young lady handed me my second beer, I screwed the top off and took my first sip. And while I was doing that I saw someone coming toward me in my peripheral vision. I turned around to see who it was, and it was Malik, the owner of the club, and two of his bouncers. I gave him a fake-ass smile and waited to hear what he had to say.

He extended his hand and welcomed me to the club. I shook his hand and thanked him for acknowledging my patronizing. But he threw me for a loop when he told me that he'd been watching me and noticed that every time

I came to his club I'd drink a couple of beers but I always avoided his dancers and never interacted with anyone in the club but his new waitress. I swear, while this guy laid out every detail of my movements in his club, I got shook. This guy made me uncomfortable. I was an agent, for God's sake. No one had ever made me feel this much anxiety in one sitting. So quite naturally I had to defuse any suspicions he may have had. But most important, I had to get the heat off Agent Zachary, because she was about to walk through those doors at any moment.

"Listen, sir, first of all, your dancers and your waitresses are gorgeous, which is why I come here. But as far as who I interact with in here is pure coincidental. I told Ms. Hollywood that she was beautiful and sexy when she asked me if I wanted a lap dance. I also told her that I was going through something personal and that I wasn't interested in a lap dance at this very moment. And if my mood started to change before I left that I would call on her personally."

"Are you sure you ain't no cop? Because you give off the vibe that you're a cop," Malik questioned me.

"No, I'm not a cop," I replied.

"Well, you know that if you are a cop and someone asks you that question, you gotta tell them the truth?"

"I think I've heard that somewhere," I told him. I tried to be as cool as I could be.

"So, you're not a cop?" Malik pressed on.

"Nope. I am not a cop," I said, trying to be as convincing as I could.

"Well, since you're not a cop, then it would be okay if I pat you down?"

Knowing that this guy wasn't going to leave me alone intensified my feeling of unease. I never traveled without my badge and my government-issued 9mm Glock. So I was in a tight spot. "Do I have any options?" I wanted to know.

"Yeah. If you want to stay here, then I have the right to search you. But if me searching you is a problem, then you're gonna have to leave my club," he told me. And from what I could see, this guy was serious.

It didn't take me long to figure out what I wanted to do. So I immediately did the latter. I placed my half-empty bottle of beer on the table, stood up, and told this guy and his henchmen to have a nice night. I was out of his club in a matter of five seconds.

"I told you that nigga was a cop," one of his bouncers blurted out.

"He's a bitch-ass nigga too!" I heard Malik comment.

They made it blatantly obvious that they wanted to start some shit with me. But I let their bogus-ass tactics go over my head. I wasn't going to let them blow my cover. I didn't need the heat.

On my way out of the club, I happened to see Agent Zachary walking toward me. And right when I was getting ready to greet her, she yelled and said, "Malik, don't tell me I'm getting a grand welcome."

I had to give it to her because she was on her A-game. The fact that she realized I was about to speak to her and prevented me from doing so by taking control of the situation, warning me that Malik was standing at the front door watching me leave, was amazing.

I heard the door of the club close after Agent Zachary greeted Malik. That was my cue to get off his property and get in my car. This way I had a little more control of my surroundings. Back in my car I immediately called Agent Humphreys while I watched a ton of men and women come and go from the club. This scene would make for a great reality show.

"Humphreys, stay by the phone, because I may need you to come out here."

"What's going on?"

"I was just escorted out of the strip club by the owner and two of his bouncers."

"What happened?"

"Either I was spotted on their cameras or someone told the owner that all the times I have come there I don't interact with the strippers and that I only dealt with his new waitress."

"He was talking about Zachary, huh?"

"Yeah, he was. So after he got through with all the preliminaries he popped the question and asked me if I was a cop. I told him no. But me telling him that I wasn't a cop didn't go over well, because a couple of seconds later he wanted to know if he could pat me down. And of course I told him that he couldn't, and that's when he told me to get out of his establishment."

"Where are you now?" Humphreys asked. He seemed alarmed by what I was saying.

"I'm outside sitting in my car watching all the traffic going in and out of the club."

"Think you might need some backup?"

"I'm good for now. But keep your phone by you just in case."

"Did Zachary see the incident between you and Malik?"

"No. She hadn't come in yet. She's in there now though."

"Do you think it's safe for her to be in there? Remember you said he knew she only dealt with you."

"Yeah, I know. But I think she'll be good. She's a smart agent. So if it gets hot in there, she'll let us know."

"Has anything else capped off out there?" Humphreys wanted to know.

"Well, so far I've only seen a few drug deals go down. Nothing big. The guys that come to this club are small-time dealers."

"Okay. But call me if you need me."

"Don't worry, I will."

I hung up with Agent Humphreys and began my surveillance outside the club, since I was kicked out of it. I looked down at my watch and realized that tonight was going to be a long night, especially since Agent Zachary just started her shift. Hopefully I'd see some action outside. I didn't want to see anyone get hurt, but any kind of entertainment among niggas from the street would do. Either the guys are standing around disrespecting women by putting their hands on them and calling them bitches or the women are getting in the men's faces and calling them deadbeats and threatening to call the police on them.

Only in America!

Chapter 18

How Will I Survive This?

Jimmy raced around the house trying to grab everything he could, because he knew that the game he was playing was about to come to an end if he didn't get out of there. With his mother gone and the only living paramedic witness having escaped, Jimmy was in a rage. He knocked over tables, chairs, lamps, and books from their makeshift bookshelf to recover money and other things of value so he could leave the house.

After he grabbed whatever he could find, he threw everything in a pillowcase and held it tightly in his right hand. With the other hand he grabbed ahold of the wheelchair I was strapped in and tried to push it, but it wouldn't budge. So he grabbed the other handle with his right hand and began to push me to the back door of the house.

Getting me out of the house and to his taxi-cab was a hard task, but he managed to do it. He opened the trunk of the cab, and before he dumped me inside he untied the straps that restrained my arms to the chair, but he left duct tape tied around my wrists. And after he cut the restraints that prevented me from moving my legs, he left the duct tape around my ankles. All he wanted to do was release me from the wheelchair. That was it. I was still bound by his fucking duct tape. I flailed and kicked and tried to scream, but my efforts proved futile.

Once I was inside he slammed the trunk of the car. I wasn't able to do anything. Trying to escape was out of the question. This fool was on a mission, and I was caught in the middle. "Mama, I'm coming to get you. I won't let any of those motherfuckers hurt you, Mama!" I heard him yelling like a maniac.

I felt all the movement when he backed the cab out of the driveway. He stepped on the brakes very suddenly and then he pressed down hard on the accelerator and sped off. I had no idea where we were going, but I knew it would be a matter of time before I did.

From a distance I heard sirens. With the screaming and yelling Jimmy was doing, the sounds faded in and out. Even though it was pitch dark in the trunk, I still closed my eyes and began a silent prayer.

I know I haven't been the best person in the world but Lord I don't deserve to die. So, please save me. And I promise I'll be the person you want me to be.

While I was praying, I still had this gut feeling that God wouldn't hear my prayer. I mean, come on. I really hadn't been a good person. I'd had a lot of people's blood on my hands, starting with my ex–best friend, who fucked my man. And then there was Duke, who was the nigga who fucked my best friend and had her turn against me. Next in line was Duke's flunkies, their baby mamas, and the innocent neighbor who was at the wrong place at the wrong time. But let's not forget Katrina, who was married to my former boss, Neeko, but had a love child by Duke and no one knew about it. I hated her ass in the beginning. But her helping me get out of her house the night Duke and his boys tried to kill me was a debt that I'd never be able to pay.

In my travels, I learned to love and hate niggas. My life had been one big, fucking mess! It seemed like bad shit always followed me. I'd never asked a nigga for shit. I'd always worked hard for my stuff. And the motherfuckers I did rob only got payback because they'd hurt me. From when I was a little girl I wanted the fairytale life all those other bitches got. I was pretty with a banging-ass body. So why was I always getting shortchanged? What was wrong with me?

While I talked to God, I noticed that my voyage with Jimmy was getting rockier and the car kept swerving from side to side. And when the sirens came within a short distance of the cab and Jimmy continued to shout more obscenities, I knew we were on a high-speed chase. "Y'all motherfuckers ain't gonna get me alive!" I heard him yell. And then I started hearing gunshots. *Bang! Bang! Bang!* That's when I knew that Jimmy was shooting at the fucking police. Was this motherfucker trying to kill me and him? "Hey, somebody's back here!" I screamed through the gag even though I knew I wouldn't be heard. I turned my body around in a way so that I could kick the door of the trunk. My main objective was to try to kick it open. "Somebody's in the trunk!" I screamed while I kicked. One part of me knew that what I was doing wasn't going to help my situation. It did, however, give me a feeling of hope that someone would hear me.

Bang! Bang! Bang! Jimmy fired three more shots at the police. This time the police returned gunshots.

Boom! Boom! Boom! Boom! Boom! The gunshots that were fired by the police had more force. In fact, one of the shots penetrated the door of the trunk. The shot missed me by less than an inch. I started going crazy. "Please!

Please! Somebody is back here! I don't want to die!" I cried.

Jimmy kept the gunfire going. *Bang! Bang! Bang!* "Y'all think y'all better than me? I'm God! Y'all can't touch me. I'm invincible!" He yelled.

Once again the cops returned gunfire. *Boom! Boom! Boom!* This time the bullets penetrated another part of the car, because before I knew it the car felt like it was in the air. I couldn't feel the road underneath the tires. And then the car started turning over and over. My body tossed and turned at least four or five times, and then the car collided into something hard. *BOOM!* My neck jerked, and I heard a cracking noise. I couldn't move an inch, because my body was twisted around and I had all my weight pressing down on my head and neck. I tried to figure out how to get out of that position, but I couldn't because my wrists were still tied together. And then out of the corner of my eye I saw flames. "Oh, my God! Somebody help me! This car is on fire!" I tried to scream, but I was still wearing the fucking gag.

I started praying again.

God, please help me. I don't want to burn up in this car. I will do anything, Lord. Please, God, help me! I can't leave this earth like this.

Even though my prayer was sincere, I knew I was about to die. So as the smoke became thicker and the flames got more intense, I started coughing uncontrollably. There was no escaping this time. That's when I stopped fighting it and closed my eyes.

Time to go and meet my maker.

Chapter 19

A Major Fucking Screwup!

Time was rolling by so freaking slow it was becoming unbearable. Normally when I did undercover stings and stakeouts, I never got this fucking bored. I had been out here for only a couple of hours. So why was I so out of it?

I turned on some music to get me by, but that did not work either. Listening to Big Sean and Drake only made me think back on my college days and all the dumb-ass chicks I used to fuck with. If I had not become an agent, I would have become a Navy Seal. What a life that would have been!

While I bumped my head to Big Sean's song "Marvin & Chardonnay," my cell phone rang. "Agent Foster," I said.

"Hi there, Agent Foster," the unfamiliar voice

said. "This is Detective Daniels from the Norfolk City Police Department."

"How are you?"

"I'm good, sir. I'm calling because I have some very bad news for you."

"What's the matter?" I asked. My heart dropped into the pit of my stomach. I knew he had to be calling me about Lynise. I mean, what else could he be calling me for?

"Is this about my witness Lynise?" I asked. My heart rate picked up speed.

"Yes, as a matter of fact, it is," the gentleman said.

"Where is she? Is she all right?" I wanted to know. This guy wasn't giving me enough information. I needed answers.

"Would it be possible for you to meet me?" he asked me.

"Yes. Of course I can. When?" I questioned him. I was anxious to find out what he knew about Lynise. Was she dead? Was she alive? Whatever it was, I needed to find out. She was my witness, and I was responsible for her.

"I'm at the DePaul Hospital on Granby Street."

"What's the address?"

"It's 4987 Granby Street. And I'll meet you inside the chaplain's office on the first floor near the emergency room entrance."

"Wait, so you're telling me she's dead?"

"Agent Foster, I'm gonna need you to come down to the hospital and we can talk then."

"Okay. I'm on my way," I told him. My heart was doing multiple flips inside my stomach. I hung up with the detective and sped off in the direction of the hospital. I called Agent Humphreys. "Humphreys, I just got a call from Detective Daniels from the Norfolk Police Department, and he wants me to meet him at the chaplain's office at DePaul Hospital at 4987 Granby Street. I'm gonna need you to be there too."

"Wait a minute, she's dead?" Humphreys wanted to know.

"He wouldn't tell me. So I'm on my way there now."

"What do you want me to tell Agents Rome and Mann?"

"Don't tell them anything. But I do want you to send them out here to the club to watch Agent Zachary's back. Tell them to leave the house now."

"Copy that."

"Don't forget to keep this mum."

"I got it," Humphreys assured me, and then we disconnected our call.

I dodged around every car on the highway to get to the hospital. I needed so desperately to find out what Detective Daniels wanted to tell me about Lynise. I prayed that she wasn't dead. But if she was, then I failed at my mission to protect her. News like that would damage me forever. I was speaking of my career as law enforcement as well as emotionally. Lynise held a special place in my heart. It felt like I may be in love.

Upon entering the emergency room my armpits and the collar of my shirt were completely drenched in sweat. The combination of anxiety and fear gripped me like a glove. I was a nervous fucking wreck!

I approached two elderly women behind the information desk. "Excuse me, ladies, can you tell me where I can find the chaplain's office?"

"Go down this hallway and make the first left turn. The chaplain's office is the second door on the right," the woman on the right said.

"Thank you so much," I told them both, and walked off.

Right before I made the first left turn, my cell phone rang. I stopped in my tracks when I noticed it was Agent Zachary's cell phone number. "Hey, Zachary, what's up?" I asked, trying not to sound overwhelmed.

"I think I've got a problem," she started off.

"What do you mean you have a problem? What's wrong?" I asked. I was taken aback, so I had to switch gears. Even though I was at the hospital en route to the chaplain's office to find out Lynise's fate, I had to regroup and find out what was going on with Agent Zachary.

"Both of the Carter brothers are here at the club right now. And the one named Terrence just approached me and asked me if I was the

woman he saw the other day driving down his
street."

"What did you say?"

"I denied it. But he didn't believe me, because after I brushed him off he walked out of
the club and then he came right back in a couple of minutes later. After he walked back into
the club, he looked at me and mumbled something to Malik. I'm thinking he went outside,
saw the rental car I was driving, and told Malik
that I lied to him."

"Damn! Why did this shit have to happen
after I left?"

"What do you mean left? You're not outside?" She panicked.

"No. I just got a call from a detective at the
Norfolk City Police Department saying he had
some information about Lynise and that I
needed to meet him at the chaplain's office on
the first floor of DePaul Hospital on Granby
Avenue."

"Are you fucking kidding me? Why didn't
you call me and tell me this? Do you realize the
danger you put me in?" she spat. She was both
angry and afraid. But did she realize that I said
I had to meet the detective inside the chaplain's office? I couldn't believe how cold-
hearted she was being.

"Look, you're gonna be fine. I just got off
the phone with Agent Humphreys. I told him
to have Agents Rome and Mann get to the
club. So they're en route to you right now."

"That's not good enough. You know I am not supposed to be left alone. We agreed that someone was supposed to have my back every minute I am here."

"I know. I'm sorry I dropped the ball." I let out a long sigh. "It's just that I got caught up by the detective's call."

"I understand all of that, but do you see what kind of position you put me in?"

"Listen, Agent Zachary, I'm sorry. Now let's move past this. I told you Agent Rome and Agent Mann are on their way to you as we speak. So what I want you to do is get the hell out of there," I warned her. She was around some very deadly men, and I feared for her life.

"Okay, let me get the keys for the rental car and then I'm gonna get out of here."

"Hurry."

"I will."

"Call me when you are on the road."

"All right."

Chapter 20

Not Giving Up

After I disconnected my call with Agent Zachary I shoved my cell phone back into the holster and proceeded toward the chaplain's office. Once again, my heart started to beat uncontrollably. Then the palms of my hands started to sweat. I needed to get a grip on myself.

I rubbed my hands across the side of my jeans to wipe off the sweat and then I let myself inside the office. There was a desk and an empty chair on the left side of the room, and a door to the right led to another room. "Hello! Is somebody here?" I yelled.

"Yes, who are you looking for?" An elderly white man with a headful of silver hair asked as he peered around the corner.

"Well, my name is Agent Foster and I was told by a detective named Daniels to meet him here."

The elderly man walked from around the corner and greeted me with a handshake. He was fully clothed in priestly garments. "Nice to meet you, sir. My name is Mr. Shultz and I am the chaplain here at DePaul Hospital."

"Nice to meet you too," I replied. I looked around the small room waiting to see if Detective Daniels was going to pop his head out too.

"It's sad how that serial killer had that poor young lady stuffed in the trunk of that burning car."

My heart crashed and burned when I heard the words *burning car*. What the hell happened? Was Lynise in fact dead? Oh, my God! I didn't think I could cope with that.

"Burning car? So, she's dead?" I uttered the words slowly. It seemed as if everything around me was going in slow motion.

Before the chaplain could answer me, I heard the office door open behind me, so I turned my head to see who it was. The chaplain smiled. "Here's Detective Daniels now," the chaplain said.

I completely turned around so I could give this detective my full attention. He was nothing like I imagined. I thought I would be meeting a tall, white stocky guy. But in fact, this guy was the exact opposite. We both extended our hands and shook. "You must be Agent Foster," the detective said. His face was blank, and I knew what that meant.

"Yes, I am. And you must be Detective Daniels," I said.

"Let's go in the back and have a seat," Daniels told me.

"Sure," I replied.

I followed the detective and the chaplain back into a seating area of the chaplain's office. The chaplain took a seat behind a desk filled with pictures of himself and other priests and with files I assumed were for patients that died in the hospital. This further crushed my hopes of Lynise being alive.

After Detective Daniels and I took a seat in the chairs placed on the opposite side of the chaplain's desk, I braced myself for the inevitable. "What's this I hear about Lynise being pulled from a burning car? Is she dead or alive? What?" I managed to say, despite the knot I had lodged in my throat. *Fuck the preliminaries! Just give me the answers I came here for.*

"She's on life support right now," Detective Daniels finally said.

"Why? What happened?" I asked. My heart felt like it was ripped from my chest abruptly.

"Well, this matter is still under investigation. But I can say that Lynise was at the residence of an alleged serial killer when the paramedics were called. One of the two paramedics was shot in the head, and the other one fled on foot. The paramedic who got away called us, and a high-speed chase started. It lasted for about five minutes and ended when the alleged serial killer lost control of his vehicle and slammed it into a tree. Immediately after the car crashed, it caught on fire. She suffered a couple of bumps and bruises. But smoke inhalation is what stopped her breathing. She had no brain waves. So she was immediately placed on life support and is currently in the intensive care unit."

"How did she get hooked up with him?"

"We don't know the answer to that yet."

"Where is the serial killer? Is he on life support too?"

"No. He suffered only minor injuries. He was placed under arrest immediately after we pulled him out of his cab."

"Wait a minute! This guy was a fucking cab driver?"

"Yep. That's what we were told."

"When did this accident happen?"

"Almost two hours ago."

"How did you know to call me?"

"When the firemen pulled her from the trunk of the cab, she had the straps of her purse holstered around her shoulder. And inside that purse was Detective Rosenberg's business card. So I called Rosenberg and wanted to know his affiliation with her, and that's when he ran everything down to me about her being held in witness protection and the meeting you guys had at the precinct when a shoot-out commenced. At the end of our conversation he gave me your cell phone number, and here we are. Oh, and speaking of Detective Rosenberg, he plans to speak with you in regards to your witness sometime later."

Instead of commenting, I buried my entire face in the palms of my hands. The news about Lynise being on life support hit me like a ton of bricks. What the fuck was I going to do now? Would she live through this? *I swear I can't lose her.*

While I was trying to cope with the fact that Lynise was depending on life support to keep her alive, I lifted my head back up. "Where is she? Can I see her now?" I asked. At this point, I needed to lay my eyes on her. Trying to imagine her state wasn't cutting it for me.

"Yes, you can see her. Come with me," Detective Daniels agreed. He stood up from his chair and exited the chaplain's office. I got up and followed him.

We walked onto the elevator and took it to the fifth floor. After we exited the elevator, we walked down a very long hallway. From there we made a right turn, and then we took a sharp left turn. During this five-story hike, Detective Daniels gave me the rundown on the security he formed for Lynise. It was refreshing to know that he cared about her safety. "I just wanted to make sure that if she recovered, she'd have the proper security to protect her, especially with the bounty I heard she had on her head. I heard she had quite a laundry list of people who wanted her head on a platter," he said, sounding like he wanted me to come back with a rebuttal. But I wasn't doing that. So instead, I took the high road.

"I really appreciate that for her," I told him.

As we approached the ICU, I counted at least seven cops standing around guarding a door that led to the room I assumed Lynise was assigned to. The closer I got to the room, the more anxiety sat in the pit of my stomach. I wanted to turn around and leave, but my heart wouldn't let me. I felt totally responsible for Lynise's situation. I figured that if I hadn't forced her to help me arrest Bishop with the federal case, she wouldn't be in this situation. But no, I wanted to be a badass and use my authority to use her as bait. Now look at her. I fucked her life up royally.

"Here we are," Detective Daniels pointed out as we approached the crowd of uniformed police officers.

I walked by the cops and peered into the window of her room. And there was Lynise, lying in the bed with gauze and bandages all over her face, while the tubes attached to a ventilator were secured to her face with tape. To see her like this was truly unbearable.

"The doctor said that it is his hope that she'll be able to breathe on her own so she can return to a normal quality of life."

"Did he say how long he'd keep her on life support?"

"No. As a matter of fact, he didn't. But I'm sure he'll be around very soon to give us all of that information."

"Can we go inside her room?"

"No. Not yet. But I'm confident that it won't be that much longer before we can."

I let out a loud sigh. "Let's hope so," I commented. I was pretty disappointed when Detective Daniels told me that we couldn't go into the room. Did he know how fucking close this woman was to me? This wasn't a fly-by-night arrangement Lynise and I had. So I needed to be next to her now.

I think I stared at Lynise through that glass for about seven minutes straight without blinking an eye. I was hurting inside and I couldn't shake it. All I could think about was how this chapter of her life is going to end.

All I could see were flatlines . . .

Chapter 21

Case Closed

The doctor for Lynise finally made himself available for Detective Daniels and I to speak with him. "So, Doctor, what can you tell us?" I spoke first.

The doctor glanced into Lynise's room and then he turned to face us. "Well, what I can say is that while she's in that coma we're gonna monitor her very closely. And who knows, she may pull through this."

"What are her chances of surviving?" I wanted to know. I needed a shot of hope from somewhere.

"It's too soon to tell," the doctor told me.

"Well, can you tell me when I'll be able to go into her room?"

"After the nurse on duty checks her vitals, then you'll be able to go inside and see her."

"Thank you," I said, and shook his hand.

As the doctor was about to leave, my cell phone rang. I looked down at the caller ID and saw that it was Agent Humphreys. I excused myself from them and stepped over into a corner so see if I could get better reception and hear what he had to say. "Humphreys, where are you?" I asked.

"I'm down on the first floor."

"Okay, well I'm on the fifth floor in the ICU. Get on the elevator near the information desk, and I'll meet you when you get off."

"Roger that," he replied.

"Daniels, my partner is on his way up, so I'm gonna meet him at the elevator."

"Sure, no problem. See you when you get back."

On my way to the elevator, my cell phone rang again. This time the call came from Agent Rome. "Hey, Rome, have you guys made it to the strip club yet?" I asked immediately after I put him on speaker.

"Yes, we're here. But we can't find Zachary."

"What do you mean you can't find Zachary? I just got off the phone with her. And I gave her specific instructions to get the hell out of that club over an hour ago." I barked. While I was I trying to make sense of what Agent Rome had just told me, I hadn't even realized I was walking around the floor in circles. Then a couple of minutes later, the elevator door opened. Agent Humphreys walked into the hallway.

"I've got Agent Rome on the phone and he's telling me that he and Agent Mann are at the strip club and Agent Zachary is nowhere to be found."

"But how can that be?" Humphreys interjected.

"I asked the same fucking question," I snapped.

"Agent Mann and I just rolled up in the club and she's not here. We even asked one of the other waitresses where she was, and she couldn't tell us," Agent Rome explained.

"Did you guys see her rental car outside in the parking lot?" I probed more.

"No. It's gone too."

"Well, have you tried calling her? Because she could be very well on her way back to the safe house." I was very agitated at this point and my tone expressed it.

"Foster, we called her over a dozen times and her phone always goes straight to her voice mail."

"This is not good. We've got to find her," I said as I continued to pace the floor.

"What do you want us to do?" Agent Rome asked.

"I want you to find her. And I don't care how you do it."

"Where do you want us to start?"

"Start with the owner, because she called me not too long ago saying that the Carter brothers were at the club and that one of them recognized her from the other day when she rode by his house. She seemed pretty spooked when he confronted her, so she denied that the woman he saw was her. But according to her, he didn't believe her and starting eyeballing her, and she began to worry that he may do something to her."

"Are you and Humphreys going to join in the search for her?"

"We're investigating a lead, so I will be in touch. But if you are able to find her before Humphreys or I call you, please call us at once."

"Will do," Rome said, and hung up.

Hearing Agent Rome tell me that he couldn't find Agent Zachary felt like a brick had slammed into my head. I was thrown off. First it was Lynise and now it is Zachary. What the fuck was I going to do?

"Sounds like we're gonna have to take a ride to the strip club," Agent Humphreys said.

"Yeah, it does." I agreed.

"Where is Lynise? And how is she?"

"They have her in ICU, which is down the hall. Her face looks pretty banged up. And they have her on life support, so she's not looking too good, at least for right now," I explained.

"What did the doctor say about her?" Humphreys's questions continued.

"He really didn't say anything but that they're gonna continue to monitor her and hope that she comes out of this."

"That's it?!"

"Yep. That's pretty much it," I said.

Chapter 22

The Witness

I escorted Agent Humphreys back to the ICU, where Detective Daniels and the cops were. I introduced Humphreys to Daniels, and we sat in a huddle talking while the nurse in Lynise's room took her vitals.

"Have you gotten any more information about the serial killer?" I blurted out.

"What serial killer?" Humphreys interjected.

"The serial killer who kidnapped Lynise."

"Well, this is what we learned. The guy's name is Jimmy.... He is a cab driver and he works in the Hampton and Newport News area. According to the cab driver's mother, who is in the hospital right now being treated for a fall, her son brought your witness to their house over a week ago. She said that her son brought her there because he wanted to marry her and start a life with her. But when the victim started talking down to him, she said he put her in her place."

"What floor is this woman on? I would sure like to speak with her," I told Daniels.

"Let's go," he agreed, and led the way.

The mother of the serial killer was lying in her hospital bed, twisting in the sheets like she was in a lot of pain. We caught her screaming obscenities at the nurse while her blood pressure was being taken. "You better hurry up and get this shit off me before I get my son on you," she threatened the woman.

"Mrs. Beckford, I will be done with you in a minute," the nurse assured her.

"You said that shit a minute ago. But you're still not done."

"That's because you keep moving your arm so I'm having to start over."

"Excuses. Excuses. I'm so tired of you fast tail girls walking around here like you're better than everybody else."

"Hi, Mrs. Beckford, my name is Detective Daniels and I have two agents with me named Foster and Humphreys."

"So what? What do you want with me?" she snapped.

"Well, we came in here to talk to you about your son, Jimmy, and maybe get you to answer some questions."

"I've already talked to another policeman. What else do you want me to say?"

"We want to talk about how your son treated the lady you guys had in your house before the paramedics brought you here."

"Well, if you think I'm going to say that I like her, you are sadly mistaken."

"What didn't you like about her?"

"She acted like she was better than my boy. And she was very disrespectful. I raised my son on the morals and values that I was raised on. I was taught that you never disrespect your elders. And I was taught that when somebody lets you into their house, you need to be grateful. And she wasn't grateful. All she did was complain about everything. She didn't appreciate anything my son did for her. And I didn't like it."

"Well, Mrs. Beckford, did Lynise come to your house voluntarily?"

"According to my son, she did. He said she flagged him down and got into his cab. And when he asked her where she was going, she told him she wanted to come home with him."

"Are you sure your son told you that?"

"Of course I'm sure. Are you calling me a liar?" she growled. She looked like she would've smacked me if I were a little closer to her.

"No, ma'am. I just want the facts. That's it," Detective Daniels said.

"Mrs. Beckford, can you tell me where Lynise got all those bruises on her face?"

"My son did it. And she deserved every bit of it."

"What did he hit her with?" I spoke up. I also had questions I needed answered.

"He hit her with his hands."

"Can you tell me why he beat her like that?"

"Have you been listening to anything I said? I told you she was being very disrespectful to me and to my son, and he was not having it. Not in our house."

"Mrs. Beckford, is your son a serial killer?"

"I beg your pardon!" she roared. I believe I went below the belt with that question, because the level of her anger went up a couple notches.

"Mrs. Beckford, do you know what a serial killer is?"

"Of course I do. I'm not stupid," she replied sarcastically.

"Well, would you please tell us what a serial killer is?" I probed more. It was obvious that this woman was a sociopath, but hearing things more than once gives you the ability to make a sound decision.

"It's a person who kills people," she answered.

"Mrs. Beckford, is your son Jimmy a serial killer?"

"No, he is not."

"Mrs. Beckford, have you ever seen your son kill someone?"

"No, I haven't."

"Mrs. Beckford, are you lying to me?"

"Who do you think you're talking to, young man? Do you know that my son will kill you if he finds out that you disrespected me? We don't stand for that type of mess."

"I'm sorry, Mrs. Beckford, we don't want that to happen."

"Well, you better mind your business before I tell him what you did," she warned me.

"Mrs. Beckford, can you tell us how many women Jimmy has brought back to your home?"

"I can't say. I don't remember," she replied, and turned her face toward the wall.

"Do you want to help your son, Mrs. Beckford?"

"What kind of stupid question is that? Of course I want to help my Jimmy."

"Well, in order to do that you're gonna have to start by telling us how many women your son brought home."

"I don't know. I lost count," she told us.

"Was it more than five?"

"Yes. More than that."

"Was it more than ten?"

"Yeah, I believe so."

"Can you give us any of the names of these women?"

"I can't recall."

"Can you tell us what some of their names start with?"

"I don't remember. Maybe one of their names was Chrissy, I think."

"Any other names?"

"I told you I don't remember."

"Will you at least try? You would be bringing closure to a lot of families if you could help," Detective Daniels said.

Mrs. Beckford lay there like she was jogging her memory. Then after about a minute she finally said, "I think I remember a woman named Maggie. That's it."

"Did Jimmy rape any of those women?"

"No, he didn't. At least not around me."

"Thank you, Mrs. Beckford," Daniels said.

"Yes. Thank you. We appreciate all your help," I chimed in, and then we all exited her room.

After having that brief chat with the serial killer's mother, we knew that Lynise had stepped into another world after she got into the taxicab with that psychopath. And to have seen a dozen TV news clips about this guy made me even angrier. How could I have let this sneak by me? I sincerely dropped the ball on this one.

"Hey, Daniels, let me have a few minutes with my partner and we'll meet you back in the ICU."

"Okay. No problem. See you guys in a few minutes," he said, and walked off.

"That shit that lady said was fucking bizarre. And to think that Lynise went through all of that shit at the hands of her son is fucking nuts."

"Yeah. That's why I'd give anything to get that motherfucker in a room by himself. I would take his life from him with one fucking blow to the head," I replied, spitting venom from my mouth.

"Calm down, Foster. We found Lynise. She's here getting the best medical treatment this place has to offer. So let's focus our energy on finding Agent Zachary."

"Yeah, you're right. It's just that she's been through a lot of shit. And what woman do you know who could put up with all the shit she's been through?"

"I can't say."

"Exactly. That's why I need just a couple of minutes with that fucking pervert so I can show him what it feels like to put his fucking hands on a woman," I growled.

"Come on, Foster. Let's get going so we can find out where Zachary is," Humphreys said as he patted me on my back.

Chapter 23

Do-or-Die

Humphreys and I went into the lounge area for families. It was empty, so we saw it as a perfect space in which to talk. "Get Rome on the phone and see if he has any news," I instructed Agent Humphreys.

I watched Humphreys as he dialed Agent Rome's cell phone number. To our surprise he didn't answer. So Humphreys dialed his number again, but there was still no answer. Then he called Agent Mann. Agent Mann answered the phone on the third ring. "Hey, Mann, what's going on? Where is Rome?" I heard Humphreys ask.

"He's inside the strip club."

"Well, that explains why he's not answering

my call. Have you guys been able to locate Agent Zachary?"

"No, we haven't. Rome is in the club talking to a few girls hoping to get a lead from them."

"What are you doing outside the club? Why aren't you in there watching his back?"

"Trust me, he's fine. He doesn't need me."

"Have you guys been able to talk to the strip club owner?"

"We tried to do that, but he had already left the club when we asked for him."

"Are the Carter brothers there?"

"No. This club is dead. There's only a few street punks inside getting lap dances and that's it. If the Carter brothers were here earlier, they're gone now."

Not at all satisfied by the work that Agents Rome and Mann were putting into find Agent Zachary, I snatched Humphreys's cell phone from him. "Hey, listen, Mann, I'm sending Humphreys out there to help you two find Zachary because what I've heard so far is unacceptable. You guys need to burn that fucking street up out there and find her."

"Foster, we're using all the resources we have."

"That excuse isn't good enough for me. I talked to her not too long ago, so she can't be that far. Now if I weren't over here at this fucking hospital looking after Lynise, I would be with you guys tearing down every door until I found our fellow agent. For all we know, she could be in fucking danger! And you're telling me you're using what resources you have? Don't ever come at me like that again, Mann, or I will have your fucking badge!" I roared. I felt like a seething predator ready to devour those lazy motherfuckers.

"All right. We'll handle it until Humphreys gets out here," Mann replied calmly.

Once I said what I had to say, I handed Humphreys his cell phone and walked away.

Humphreys disconnected the call and ran behind me to catch me before I got back on the elevator. "You know you just told Mann that you were here at the hospital, right?"

"Yes, I realized that, but at this point I don't even care. Those guys are fucking lazy! And I can't take it."

"Well, you know that he's going to tell Rome the news?"

"Like I said, at this point I couldn't really care less. I've got too much shit to worry about than to sweat over those two jerk-offs! They're a big fucking joke. And as soon as we get back to New Jersey, I'm switching their details to another unit."

"You know you're gonna open up a can of worms if you do that?"

"And that's what I want," I replied sarcastically, and then I turned away from Humphreys and walked toward the elevator. "Be careful out there. And call me as soon as you get any new developments," I instructed him.

Just like that, I got one elevator going up. He got on the other elevator going down to the first floor. With Agent Humphreys handling Agent Zachary's detail, I felt like I could concentrate on Lynise and her recovery. It felt like a load was lifted.

On the way up to the fifth floor all I thought about was that Lynise would have a speedy recovery and then we could leave this place. I was taking her back to New Jersey. Better yet, I'd relocate with her. I had to have her in my life. And if that meant that I had to resign, then so be it.

Chapter 24

Life

We were finally given the green light to go into Lynise's room. Detective Daniels encouraged me to go in the room first, out of respect of course. But immediately after I stepped inside and closed the door, a weird feeling came over me. Seeing her lying in the bed like that was eerie. She looked like she was dead. I wanted so badly to get Detective Daniels to accompany me, but I decided against that. I figured I'd look like a fucking wimp asking another man to stand by my side while I visited a woman whom I'd fucked and was chosen to protect. Talk about sheer embarrassment.

I walked up to her bed and looked at her from head to toe. I examined her face and her arms, all while thinking about why that fucking serial killer beat her like that. Lynise was really fucked up. Not only did he alter her facial features, he also caused her to be on life support. I wished I could see that bastard. I'd kill him on the spot. No questions asked.

After I checked out every inch of her body, I sat in the chair placed next to her bed and wondered if she'd ever come out of this. I also wondered if she'd go back to her old ways if she recovered. I guessed time would tell.

I sat there and tried to think of the good things that she and I did together. I even thought back to when she and I had our first unofficial date. Those times were good. So I reasoned that if I could think about the good times Lynise and I had, then God would spare her life and bring her back to me. And I promised that this time I wouldn't ever take my eyes off her.

While I reminisced, I heard two knocks on the door. "Who is it?" I asked.

"Detectives Whitfield and Rosenberg. Can we come in?" Rosenberg replied.

"Sure, come on in."

Both men entered the room. I noticed that Detective Daniels stayed in the hallway.

I stood up to greet them. "How is everything, gentlemen?" I said.

"We were hoping you'd tell us," Detective Rosenberg said.

I sat back down. "Let's just say it's the same shit but on a different day."

"How is she coming along?" Rosenberg asked.

"Everything's steady. But she'll pull through."

Detectives Rosenberg and Whitfield walked up to Lynise's bed to get a closer look. "Can you tell me why she always gets hooked up with the wrong people?" Rosenberg asked.

Shocked by his comment, I asked him to repeat himself. "What the fuck did you just say?" I barked.

"Look, Foster, I didn't come in here to rain on anyone's parade," Rosenberg commented.

"So then what do you call it?" I raised my voice. This guy was walking on thin ice.

Detective Whitfield interjected. "What he's trying to say is that your witness isn't what you think she is."

"Don't you two think that this is not the appropriate time to talk about her character? I mean, geesh . . . she is lying here in a fucking coma!" I snapped.

"Sounds like you've gotten a little too attached," Detective Rosenberg chimed in. "I mean, isn't that a violation of a federal agent's code of conduct?"

I got back to my feet. "Just what are you insinuating?" I barked. I was standing on one side of the bed, and Rosenberg and Whitfield were standing on the opposite side.

Whitfield looked at me while he placed his arm in front of Rosenberg. "We're not getting anywhere by doing this," he said.

"You need to address that shit to your partner!" I roared.

By this time Detective Daniels had stormed into the room. "What's going on, guys?" he said.

"Detective Daniels, escort these fucking creeps out of here before I call marshall law on their ass!" I replied sarcastically.

"Oh, so now you're a tough guy?!" Detective Rosenberg challenged me. The motherfucker was trying to test my patience.

Detective Daniels threw up his arms. "Calm down, gentlemen! This is not the time or the place to be doing this."

"Detective Daniels, please walk these half-ass cops out of here before I get Obama to shut this hospital down," I spat. I was fucking pissed about how these local-ass cops were treating me, which is why I threw President Obama's name out there. I never had a conversation with the president, nor had I ever been in his presence, but it felt good to name-drop. These guys' faces looked like shit afterward.

"All right, detectives, let's exit the room," Detective Daniels instructed them.

I smiled. "See you later, gentlemen," I said.

"Oh, don't worry, we will see you and your witness as soon as we can prove that she is tied to the murders of her best friend and Duke Carrington," Rosenberg hissed.

"And we'll be waiting," I barked. I wasn't fazed by their idle threats. Those two small-time cops had no authority or jurisdiction over

Lynise, and I would make sure it stayed that way.

After those two left the room, Detective Daniels sprung a few questions my way. "I'm sorry that had to happen right now. But I've got to ask, do you think that there's some validity to those accusations?"

"Detective Daniels, I am not naive. Of course I have some concerns about her involvement in those murders. But I can't entertain that right now, because for one, she's lying in this bed fighting for her life. And two, she's my witness for a much bigger case. So, my advice for those play cops that just left the room is, Do your job. That's your case. Don't bring that shit to me."

"I can understand where you're coming from with that," he agreed.

"Thank you. I really appreciate that," I told him.

Detective Daniels and I chatted about thirty minutes, but then it ended when my cell phone started ringing. I asked him if he'd watch Lynise while I took the call in the hallway. He obliged.

"Hello," I said as I walked into the hallway.

"Hey, Foster, we've got a problem," Agent Humphreys said. His voice didn't sound right.

"What's wrong now?" I snapped. It seemed like everything was falling apart all around me.

"I'm over here at the strip club and I don't see anyone. Agent Zachary's rental isn't here, and neither are Agents Rome and Mann."

"Have you tried to call them?"

"Yes, I've tried to call them over a dozen times. But they won't pick up."

"Have you asked anyone there if they've seen them?" I mean, it's not like the fucking strip club is three stories tall. You can walk through the entire club and it would only take two minutes to do it.

"Yeah, as a matter of fact, I have. I asked a few of the waitresses if they seen them, and they said they saw them talking to Malik about twenty minutes ago. I also asked them when they last saw the new waitress, and they said that she left in her car like she was in a rush."

"Damn! This cannot be happening," I said.

"So what do you want me to do now?"

"I want you to keep trying to get Rome and Mann on the phone. Call Agent Zachary's cell phone too. I'm gonna also do that on my end, but if you don't make any headway, then get back over to the hospital."

"Okay," he said. Right when I was getting ready to disconnect our call, Agent Humphreys blurted out, "Hey, Foster, I think I just saw Rome and Mann's car."

"Where was it?"

"It just rode by the parking lot of the strip club."

"Go catch them and call me back after you speak with them. I need to know what the fuck is going on!"

"Will do."

Detective Daniels approached me in the hallway immediately after I ended my call. "Got a moment?" he asked me.

"Yeah, sure. What's up?" I replied.

"I just wanted you to know that I'm about to get out of here and head back to the office. I've got a few things to do before the night's over."

"Oh, okay. That's understandable. Take care of your business."

"Is there anything you need before I leave?" Detective Daniels wanted to know.

"No. I'm good. I'm just gonna stick around here for the rest of the night."

"Are your agents gonna come back?"

"Yes, they're on their way back here as we speak," I lied. I couldn't let this man know how fucked up my partners were. Our unit had become so disorganized it was pathetic.

"Okay. Well, I'm gonna have two of my uniformed officers stick around until your agents get back. Is that all right with you?"

"I'd really appreciate that."

"It's done. If you need anything, don't hesitate to call me. I keep my cell phone on all night."

"Sounds great. Thanks, detective."

"No problem," he said as we shook hands.

He left two of his officers instructions, then the other three cops followed him to the elevator. I waved them off and headed back to Lynise's room.

I took a seat back in the chair beside her bed

and started massaging her left arm. Her body was warm, and it felt good touching her, especially after giving up hope that I'd never see her again. This was a triumphant moment for me. She was now safe and sound. And I vowed that no one else would ever take her from me again.

I'd die first before I let anyone hurt her.

Chapter 25

Going Out With a Bang!

An hour went by, and the nurse on duty was back in Lynise's room to check her vital signs again. She must've seen the sadness in my eyes when I looked at Lynise, because she spoke about it.

"Don't look so sad," she said.

"Is it that noticeable?" I asked her.

"Yes, it is. But I also see how much you love her too."

I got choked up when she recognized the love I had for Lynise. I really didn't know how to respond to it. So I said nothing and smiled.

"How long have you two been married?" she continued to question me.

"We're not married," I told her.

She smiled back. "You mean, you're not married yet?"

I smiled once again. "Are you psychic?" I joked, trying to make light of the situation.

"I've had people ask me that." She cracked another smile.

"Well, all I can say is, you're good," I replied, and looked back down at Lynise. "Do you think she'll come back?"

"I can't say for sure. But I've seen a lot of cases where the patient did come back."

"On the average, how long did it take?"

"Well, it can happen as soon as a few days, and then I've seen some cases where it took months. It just all depends on the patient."

"What would make her chances good?"

"That's kind of hard to say. There is really nothing that anyone can do at this point. Just sit there and continue to talk to her. Who knows, she may be able to hear you."

"Thank you. I really appreciate what you're doing for her."

"No problem. That's what I am here for."

While the nurse continued to work on Lynise, my cell phone rang again. I looked down at the caller ID screen and saw Agent Humphreys's number come up on the screen. I knew I couldn't take the call in the room, so I got up to leave. "Will you please excuse me for a moment?" I asked her.

"Sure," she replied.

When I got into the hallway I walked by the

two police officers standing outside the door and headed to the other end of the hall. I needed as much privacy as I could get. "Humphreys, got some news for me?" I asked the second I pressed down on the send button and placed the phone up to my ear.

"We got a problem," Humphreys said.

"I'm so sick of hearing about all these fucking problems we have. When are we going to fix something? And where the hell are Agents Rome and Mann? Did you catch up with them?" I growled. I was over all of this bullshit!

"No. That car I saw wasn't theirs."

"Have you found out where Agent Zachary is?"

"That's what I want to talk to you about."

"Well, talk."

"I can't. Not over the phone. It's too risky."

"Well, then how do you want to talk about it?"

"I'm about three minutes away from the hospital now. Meet me outside in the parking lot of the emergency room."

"Okay. I'm on my way down there now."

"All right."

Out of common courtesy I told the cops that I was going out of the hospital for a couple of minutes and that I needed them to keep a watchful eye as they guarded Lynise while I was gone. They assured me that they'd take care of her. So I raced down to the first floor.

A gust of wind hit me after I exited the hospital. It was a breath of fresh air. Then I started thinking about how we take shit like this for granted. I can say that this brief experience definitely made me appreciate the little things.

I admired the solace of nature, but I quickly snapped back into reality when I noticed Agent Humphreys's car drive up. As he parked his car, I started walking in his direction. By the time I got within arm's distance of the car, the driver's side door opened. "I can't wait to hear this bullshit you're about to lay on me," I said.

"Oh, I doubt that very seriously," an unfamiliar voice said, and then out popped the head of the strip club owner, Malik. A second and a half later the back door window rolled down, but I couldn't see a thing until the barrel of a pistol, with a silencer attached, reared its ugly head. I didn't know whether to pull out my pistol or run for my life.

"What can I do for you, gentlemen?" I asked. I was nervous as hell, but I kept my cool.

"You thought you'd never see my face again, huh?"

"I actually never thought about it."

"Well, can you tell me why you lied to me about being a cop?"

"I'm not a cop."

"Oh, nigga, don't play games with me. If you walk around with a pistol and a badge, then you're a cop."

"Well, I can't argue with you on that point," I said, trying to act as calmly as I possibly could. I couldn't see who was in the backseat pointing that gun at me, but I knew I would find out sooner than later.

"So we heard that our girl Lynise is upstairs lying in one of those hospital beds. Do you want to confirm that for us?" Malik asked.

"Yeah, she's up there, but she was just transferred down to the morgue," I lied.

"That's bullshit and you know it!" Malik snapped.

"No. I'm serious. She just died a little under an hour ago."

"What floor is she on?"

"Listen, I don't know what floor she's—" I started to say, but I was cut off midsentence when Malik yelled at me.

"Shut up! Let's see if this will change your mind. Let him out of the car."

Before I could blink an eye, Agent Humphreys stepped out of the backseat with that same pistol and silencer pointed at his head. Holding the gun was Terrence Carter, the same guy who questioned Agent Zachary after she passed his home. So I knew this wasn't good.

"Hey, listen, you guys, if we can put down the gun, I'm sure we can handle this situation in a manner that would benefit us all."

"The only thing that would benefit me is for me to get my hands on your witness," TC commented.

"Wait, how did you know that Lynise was my witness?" I wanted to know.

"The female cop you sent in to spy on my cousin Malik told us everything."

"Where is she?"

"Oh, don't worry about her. She's sound asleep."

"What did you do to her?"

"I didn't do anything. You did it when you sent her in and left her all alone."

"That's bullshit! Tell me what you did to her!"

"It's too late for her. Let's focus on this gentleman right here," he said as he turned his attention back to Agent Humphreys.

I looked into Humphreys's eyes and could tell that he was sorry that he brought these guys here. So I had to let him know that it was okay. "Hey, buddy, it's all right," I spoke up.

"Oh no. It's not all right until I say it's all right," TC roared. "Now tell me where Lynise is before I blow his fucking head off!" he yelled. I knew his patience was about to run out.

"Foster, he already knows where she is. He just wanted you away from her room. He's got four guys in there right now looking for her so they can kill her!" Agent Humphreys yelled. And before I could open my mouth, TC fired the gun twice at Humphreys's head. Humphreys's eyes rolled to the back of his head and his body went limp. TC released his grip on Humphreys, and he fell to the ground. Life was sucked out of me seeing my partner fall dead right before my eyes. First they killed Agent Zachary, now

Agent Humphreys. I had to stop them once and for all.

I grabbed my pistol from my side and ducked down on the ground. I had to take cover to prevent myself from being shot, and then I let off three shots. *BOOM! BOOM! BOOM!* I heard shots being fired at me too. They were trying their best to keep me out here. But I couldn't let that happen. I had to get out of here. Lynise needed me.

After firing four more shots, I managed to run. I ducked behind a few cars before I was able to enter the hospital through another entry. "He's getting away!" I heard Malik scream.

As soon as I got into the hospital, I ran into a janitor and asked him to call the police. "Tell them to get to ICU now. They're at least four guys up there right now trying to kill the patient on life support in room 5Q," I said, panting. I was literally out of breath. But that didn't stop me from getting the word out, because I had no one left to back me. Agent Zachary and Agent Humphreys were dead, and Agents Rome and Mann were nowhere to be found.

Instead of taking the elevator, I ran up all five flights of steps. When I reached the fifth floor, I reloaded my ammo. I opened the door to the fifth-floor stairwell and peered into the hallway. At that moment, I heard a whole bunch of screaming and gunshots being fired, so I had no idea what I was up against. I was sure that TC and Malik had already warned his boys that I was on my way back to the room, so I also knew that I had to be very precise when I made my move.

My heart started beating rapidly after I entered into the hallway. With every turn I made, I pushed myself against the wall before I made my next move. "Come on, Foster, you gotta save her," I said in a whisper. I counted to the number three and then I moved down and peeped around the corner. "Fuck!" I hissed. My heart rate tripled when I saw all of the hospital staff lying in pools of blood. I knew that there was no way I was going to see Lynise alive after this.

Still panting, I very carefully moved down the hallway with the hopes that I wouldn't be seen.

"Check every room until you find her." I heard a voice that sounded like TC. So I moved closer to where his voice was coming from. I held my finger on the trigger, waiting to fire it. I had to step over six bodies before I was able to put a face with the voice. And just as I had suspected, TC and Malik, along with four more men, were ransacking the entire fifth floor.

"Put your hands up!" I heard men say in unison.

I looked to my right and saw at least ten policemen with riot gear pointing their pistols at TC and his boys. But those guys weren't going down without a fight. They raised their

guns and started a shoot-out with all ten cops.
BANG! BANG! BANG!

*BOOM! BOOM! BOOM! BOOM! BOOM!
POP! POP! POP!*

*BANG! BANG! BANG! BANG! POP! POP!
POP!*

It was sheer pandemonium. They put a couple of bullets inside Malik and two of the guys with him, so it was lights out for them. From the looks of it, the cops were handling their own, so I decided to go find Lynise.

I crawled to get out of harm's way until I was completely out of sight. Then I got to my feet and walked quietly in the direction of Lynise's room. I moved carefully to the next hallway, which was where her room was. After I stopped, peered around the corner, and saw that the coast was clear, I moved up quickly. I didn't see the two police officers who were supposed to be guarding her. The hallway was completely deserted. Realizing this made my heart fall to the pit of my stomach. I didn't know whether this was a good sign or a bad one. I held my breath as I crawled over to her room, and when I stood to look inside, I saw that Lynise was lying there unharmed. I rushed into the room, but when I tried to lock the door, TC stood there before me and let off the first shot through the window. The window shattered, and I dove to the floor.

"Yeah, you took me right to her! You dumb-ass cop!" TC roared as he kicked in the door of Lynise's room. "My brother is going to be very pleased when he finds out that I finally found the bitch that ruined our multimillion-dollar adoption enterprise," TC growled as he aimed the gun at Lynise.

I jumped up from the floor and dove onto Lynise's bed as TC fired one shot after the next. I felt every bullet that went through me. But that didn't matter to me. Lynise was my main concern. So if it meant that I had to die for her, then so be it.

"Put your weapon down!" I heard a cop yell.

I knew he was talking to TC, but I couldn't turn my head to see. I was weak and I felt the movement in my body slowly deteriorating. Within the next few seconds I heard another ten shots fired. "He's down," I heard one of the cops say. While that was good for me to hear, I knew that wasn't enough to keep me alive. TC had already shot me four times. It felt like he hit some important organs. My blood was rushing from me like water from a running faucet. I searched Lynise's face closely to see if she was still breathing, and when I heard the sounds of the life support monitor, my hope was confirmed. All I could do was lay my head down on her chest. Leaving this world lying next to her was all I needed. I looked at Lynise for the final time, and then I closed my eyes.

Hopefully, I'd see her on the other side . . .

Chapter 26

Come Into The Light

Beep. Beep. Beep. I awoke to the sounds of hospital machines in my ears. And when I opened my eyes, I saw Agent Sean lying sideways across my chest. I blinked my eyes because I thought I was dreaming. "We need assistance in room 5Q. Agent is down with gunshot wounds to the chest. He is coughing up blood, and we need an IV," I heard one nurse yell.

"What is his blood pressure?" a doctor asked.

"It's dropping," another woman yelled.

"He is losing consciousness. We need to get this man to surgery," the same doctor yelled.

Hearing all of this commotion led me to believe that I really was dreaming. When my vision became clear, I realized that my hospital room was surrounded by the agents and nurses. Then

I saw most of them push a gurney out of my room.

"What's going on?" I managed to say.

None of the officers would answer me. A nurse stepped up toward me.

She was an elderly white woman. "You can relax. We're taking care of things," she said.

"Taking care of what? And why is all this blood on me? Is this my blood?" I asked her in haste. I blinked my eyes, hoping that I was seeing things.

An unfamiliar agent stepped up by the nurse while she was cleaning the blood off me.

"Lynise, my name is Agent Mills, and I have been assigned to be with you until you leave the hospital," he told me.

"But where is Agent Sean? He's supposed to be with me. All the rest of y'all cops are dirty. Y'all don't give a fuck about me!" I screamed.

"Just calm down, ma'am," the nurse instructed me.

"No, I'm not calming down for shit! Where is Sean? I wanna see him now."

"Sir, I'm sorry but I'm gonna have to ask you to step away from the patient," the nurse ordered the agent.

"Where is Agent Sean?" I screamed again.

Agent Mills stood by my bed as if he wasn't going to move one inch. Two other agents stood on the other side of my room like they were there to protect him and not me.

"Lynise, if you calm down, then I'll be able

to answer your question." Agent Mills spoke again. He gave the impression that he was in charge and I was going to have to deal with it.

Before I spoke again, I looked down at the sheets as the nurse continued to remove them. "Is that my blood?" I asked her once again.

"No, it's not," she finally answered me.

Her words were swirled around in my head, which made me look around the room, and that's when I noticed another puddle of blood on the floor. "Is that my blood on the floor?" I asked her.

"No, ma'am," she replied.

"Then whose blood is it?" I pressed on.

"Lynise, we will answer all of your questions momentarily. Right now we need to ask you a few questions of our own."

"What . . . what . . . do you people want from me?" I rasped out. My throat felt like I had eaten a bag of gravel. My voice sounded like it too.

"We need to ask you some questions about the Carter brothers and Bishop," Agent Mills replied. I could see deep concern lacing his face with wrinkles. His white bald head glistened with sweat too. He seemed to be nervous. Finally it all came together. I knew what I needed to do now. I needed to tell them everything so that they could make some more arrests and make themselves look good in front of the media.

"I . . . I . . ." I started to say, but my words

were cut off abruptly. My eyes went wide, and the heart monitors starting ringing as my heart pounded in my chest. "I ain't got shit to say to y'all motherfuckers!" I spat. "I can't trust any one of y'all fake-ass cops. All of y'all are out for one thing, and that's get the bounty that's on my head," I continued.

"Lynise, I can promise you that that won't happen again," Agent Mills spoke.

"You can't promise me shit! Do you know how many times I've been shot at? Do you know how many attempts have been on my life?

"You're a fucking lie! You don't know shit about me! All you know is that a bunch of your agents are on the Carter brother's payroll and you are looking really stupid in the public's eye. But guess what? I'm gonna continue to let you motherfuckers look stupid, because I'm not saying another word. Now tell me, Where the hell is Agent Sean?!" I yelled. My insides became hot, and my heart monitor was screaming with beeps. I squinted at him and pushed him away from me. He looked shocked by my sudden dismissal, but I'm sure he could figure out why by then.

"Why won't you get it through your head that I don't want any of y'all in here? Y'all are the biggest liars and fakest cops that I know!" By this time, my heart monitors were making crazy noises as my blood pressure and heart rate sped up.

"Get the fuck out of my room! I only want Agent Sean in here," I choked out.

"I'm sorry to inform you, but Agent Foster is in surgery right now fighting for his life. So do you want all of his work to be in vain? Tell us what we are dealing with so we can finish this manhunt once and for all," Agent Mills replied.

"What do you mean he's in surgery fighting for his life?! That's a lie and you know it. Y'all just don't want him working on my case anymore. Y'all know that he really loves me so he's trying to separate us! I see right through your bullshit! Get away from me!! Get away from me!! I hate you! I hate you!" I screeched so loudly I scared myself.

"Don't do this, Lynise. You have to help us before more people are killed. I'm begging you to listen to the law for once in your life. Trust that I know everything that needs to be done to protect you," the agent tried to assure me.

The nurse stepped in between Agent Mills and my bed. "Let's go, gentlemen. You have to leave right now," the nurse ordered them.

"No! You are a liar!" I barked. The damn nerve of this fucking agent. He doesn't know me like Agent Foster. Tears started draining out of the sides of my eyes and pooling in my ears. The thought of Agent Sean fighting for his life had officially broken my heart. I didn't know if I could ever recover if he died.

"Get away from me! I don't want any of you

around me right now! Get away! You don't know what's best for my life. Only Agent Sean does," I cried out as loud as I could. "All of y'all are fucking monsters who have no regard for human life!"

As if I had pushed some magical button on his brain, the agent finally walked away from me. After he and the other agents left my room, I looked at the nurse and asked her if Agent Sean was really in surgery fighting for his life. And when she told me that he was in fact in surgery, my heart sunk completely into the pit of my stomach. How could that be? He can't leave me here to fight these people all by myself. *Does he know that they will devour me?*

DON'T MISS

The Mark by Kiki Swinson

In the explosive follow-up to her high-octane The Score, *a master thief's ultimate payday delivers the deadliest game of all . . .*

Conspiracy by De'nesha Diamond

Bestselling author De'nesha Diamond brings her dynamic storytelling talent to D.C.'s treacherous corridors of power—where scandal is merely the first move in a high-stakes game that makes its own rules . . .

Available wherever books are sold.

From *The Mark*

Chapter 1

I Messed with
the Wrong Guy

I can't believe I finally got the life I've always
wanted. It seemed like it was yesterday when I
left Virginia from a life of crime. Even though I
was on the run, I met and married the man I love
and finally have a baby. No one would've ever
told me that I was going to leave Matt, the hustler I'd been with since forever, after all he and
I had been through. But him screwing around
on me with Yancy changed everything. Taking
all the money that he, Yancy, and I stole was
the best revenge plot I could've ever mustered

up. It felt good to be the last woman standing. It also helped me that after I ran off with the money, Matt and Yancy both got arrested. But Matt wasn't away for long.

Now here I was in my hospital room, looking at a man I'd hoped to never see again. I'd just delivered my baby boy and everything was supposed to be right in my world. But here he is, turning my dreams for the future into a nightmare. After Matt told me he had a couple of people on the outside pay off a couple COs on the inside to help break him out of jail in exchange for some of the $3 million payout, I watched as he walked out of the hospital room with my baby in tow. My entire body cringed at the sight of him holding my infant baby. There was nothing I could do that would calm me down and quell the alarming fear that flitted through my stomach right then. "Matt," I sobbed, barely able to speak. "Please . . . don't do this."

"Do what? Take your son like you took my motherfucking money?" he chuckled wickedly. I crinkled my eyebrows in response. He stopped laughing abruptly and started talking in a very serious tone. "Bitch, I want back every fucking dime you took from me. And just know that if you don't come off it, you will be making funeral arrangements for this little motherfucker right here," he barked. His words sunk in on me and I felt hopeless. I didn't know what the fuck

I was going to do, but I knew I had to come up with his money or else.

The thought of him mishandling or mistreating my baby made me sick to my stomach. Thankfully, he grabbed a few Pampers and bottles of formula to carry along with him. I cried silently, avoiding any unwanted attention. But I knew that if I stayed around here much longer, either the doctors or nurses would know something was wrong after they found out my baby was nowhere around.

Still somewhat medicated, I got up on shaky legs, but I couldn't let that deter me from getting out of there. I got dressed pretty fast and managed to walk out of the hospital without being detected by the staff who were assigned to treat me.

When I arrived downstairs on the main floor, my body felt hot all over. I felt like I could just faint. But I pressed on and got into the first taxi I saw. I gave him my home address, sat back in the seat, and tried to pull myself together. I couldn't help but wonder whether Matt really had Derek like he insinuated, so I called his cell phone and prayed that he'd answer it. My call was picked up on the second ring. "Hello," I rushed to say.

All I got was laughter on the other end. The laughter came from Matt's voice. "Matt, where is Derek?" I asked. I was completely irritated by his insensitive behavior.

"I already told you where he was. Didn't you believe me?" he replied.

"I wanna speak to him now. I need to know if he's all right," I demanded.

"Hold on. Let me see if he's available." Matt continued his laughter.

The cell phone went silent for five long seconds. Then I heard my husband's voice. "Hello, Lauren, is this you?" Derek asked.

"Yes, baby, it's me. Are you all right?" I whined desperately. I needed answers and I needed them now.

"Yes, I'm fine."

"What about the baby? Is he all right? Has he been crying?"

"He's fine. He's drinking his bottle now," Derek replied, his voice sounding weary.

"Baby, don't worry. I'm gonna get you and our baby out of this okay," I tried to assure him.

"Now that's the spirit I like! Save your man and your baby!" Matt interjected. When I heard his voice, I knew that he had taken the phone from Derek.

"If you put your fucking hands on any one of them, I promise you'll fucking regret it!" I roared. I knew I couldn't actually speak of the money in front of the taxi driver nor the gun I was going to bring along with me when I finally met up with Matt to make the switch, so I said the next best thing. Matt knew what I meant.

"You only have twenty-four hours! So call me as

soon as you pick up the money," he demanded, and then the call went dead.

Hearing Matt's usual warning play in my ears now made a huge lump in the back of my throat. Tears sprang up to my eyes, but I fought to keep them from falling. I couldn't let anyone know what was going on with me concerning Matt and my family. Letting someone know would be too risky. And I couldn't let anything happen to my family.

I swallowed hard and closed my eyes because I knew he wasn't going to let this go. I had to think quickly. This thing had gone from complicated to nightmarish. I was now responsible for two lives. Lives of two people I loved dearly.

I swear I blanked out after Matt disconnected our call. I had no idea I had arrived at my apartment building until the taxi driver announced it to me for the second time. "Ma'am, we are here at your destination," the taxi driver said.

I looked at the cabdriver and then I looked out the back-door window and realized that he was absolutely right. I was home, so I needed to pay him and continue on with my mission. I reached into my purse, grabbed thirty dollars, and paid him. Before he could give me my five dollars in change, I had already gotten out of the car and closed the door.

My family's life meant more to me than fucking five dollars. I walked into my apartment building as fast as I could, considering the amount of drugs I had in my system. The building doorman spoke to me upon opening the door. I spoke back without giving him eye contact. He knew I had been in the hospital to have the baby, so he made mention of it. "Ms. Kelly, where's the bundle of joy?" he asked cheerfully.

"He's still in the hospital with his dad," I yelled back without turning around. But the questions didn't stop there. He must've noticed the pain I was in when I walked by him because he asked me if I needed any help. "No, I'm good," I continued. I couldn't get on the elevator and away from that meddlesome doorman soon enough. As badly as I needed help to deal with getting my family back, I knew the doorman wouldn't be cut out for the job.

Thankfully, the elevator was empty when I got on it. When the elevator doors dinged open, the reality that Matt had resurfaced in my life had become a permanent fixture in my mind. I rushed through the elevator doors and sped down the long, carpeted hallway that led to my apartment. The hallway was pin-drop quiet as usual. In a ritzy building like that it was the norm. Although it was quiet and empty, I was looking around like a burglar about to rob someone's house; that is how nervous I felt. I don't know if I was nervous about going in my apartment or nervous about someone being there after I opened up the door.

THE MARK

My heart jerked in my chest as I reached down to unlock my door. Before I pushed the door open, I looked around again, paranoid that someone was watching me. But why? That damn hallway was empty as hell. So I pushed the door open and walked inside. Immediately after I closed the door and locked it, my mind was racing at an unbelievable speed. Trying to hatch a plan to get the money and get my baby and my man back was becoming a little more than I could bear. Deep down in my heart I knew I couldn't fuck this up. The depth of hatred that Matt had for me was indescribable. Not only had I robbed him of the heist he and I crafted together, I'd also left him and started another family. At this very moment, I needed to focus solely on giving Matt what he wanted. And if I didn't deliver the goods to him within twenty-four hours, I knew my family would die.

"Come on, Lauren, you can do this, baby girl," I started telling myself. I needed as much pep talk as I could get. "Get yourself together and go down to this bank and get that money so you can get your man and your baby back. They're all you have in this world. Fuck that money! Let that sorry-ass nigga have it. He needs it more than you."

I looked over at the clock on the DVR and noticed that I didn't have a lot of time before the bank closed. With my bank being ten blocks away from my apartment, I knew I had to hurry up, change clothes, and hop in the first taxi I saw. My family's lives depended on me.

On my way to my bedroom I had to walk past my baby's nursery. Derek and I designed this room ourselves. It was Derek's idea to paint the room blue, white, and yellow. But I picked out the thin-blue-striped wallpaper. His room was simply gorgeous. So when I entered it, my heart dropped at the sight of his empty, white, laced bassinette. Seconds later, tears formed and started falling from my eyes. Next thing I knew, I had broken down and started crying. All of the emotions I was feeling from the kidnapping consumed me. My baby wasn't supposed to be with Matt. He was supposed to be here with Derek and me. "God, please help me get my baby back!" I cried out after I fell down to my knees. "Lord, please don't let anything happen to my baby. He needs me, God! So please let me get him back safely. And I promise I will surrender my life totally to you, Lord!" I ended my prayer.

I think I wallowed in my sorrows for another ten minutes before I snapped out of it. Remembering I now had less than fifty minutes to dress and get the money got me back on my feet and focused. I wanted to take a shower but I couldn't. I didn't have enough time. Nor did I have the energy, so I took off everything I had on and slipped on a pair of dark brown cargo pants with pockets along the leg. Then I slipped on an old brown flannel shirt, two pairs of socks, a pair of tan Timberland boots, and a camou-flage-designed cargo jacket. I looked like I was ready for war, but my body felt otherwise.

I looked back at the clock on the DVR and saw that another ten minutes had gone by. Panic-stricken, I grabbed an old backpack Derek owned that was on the floor of the hall closet. And then I grabbed his gun from the lockbox that was hidden in the back of the closet but on the top shelf. I wasn't going anywhere without it.

After I placed the pistol inside the backpack, I grabbed my house keys and two forms of ID from my purse and shoved all three items down inside the right front pocket of my pants. I was ready to get back what belonged to me and I was willing to risk my life to do it.

From *Conspiracy*

Chapter 1

Washington, D.C
Winter

Ascared and hungry fourteen-year-old Abrianna Parker stepped out of Union Station and into the dead of night. The exhilaration she'd felt a mere hour ago evaporated the second D.C.'s blistering wind sliced through her thin leather jacket and settled somewhere in her bones' marrow. A new reality slammed into her with the force of a ton of bricks—and left her reeling.

"Where is he?" she whispered as she scanned the growing crowd. Abrianna was more than an hour late to meet Shawn, but it couldn't have been helped. Leaving her home had proved to be much harder than she'd originally realized. After several close calls, she'd managed to escape the house of horrors with a steel determination to never look back. Nothing could ever make her return.

Now it appeared that she'd missed her chance to link up with her best friend from school, or rather they used to go the same high school, before Shawn's father discovered that he was gay, beat the hell out of him, and then threw him out of the house. Miraculously, Shawn had said that it was the best thing to have ever happened to him. Over the past year, he'd found other teenagers like him living out on the streets of D.C. His eclectic group of friends was better than any blood family, he'd boasted often during their frequent text messages.

In fact, Shawn's emancipation from his parent had planted the seeds in Abrianna's head that she could do the same thing. Gathering the courage, however, was a different story. The prospect of punishment, if she was caught, had paralyzed her on her first two attempts and had left Shawn waiting for her arrival in vain. Maybe he thought she'd lost her nerve tonight as well. Had she thought to charge her battery before leaving the house, she would be able to text him now to find out where he was.

Abrianna's gaze skimmed through the hustle and bustle of the crowd, the taxis and cars. Everyone, it seemed, was in a hurry. Likely, they wanted to meet up with family and friends. It was an hour before midnight. There was a certain kind of excitement that only New Year's

Eve could bring: the tangible *hope* that, at the stroke of midnight, everyone *magically* changed into better people and entered into better circumstances than the previous year.

Tonight, Abrianna was no different.

With no sight of Shawn, tears splashed over Abrianna's lashes but froze on her cheeks. Despite a leather coat lined with faux fur, a wool cap, and leather gloves, Abrianna may as well have been butt-ass naked for all the protection it provided. "Goddamn it," she hissed, creating thick frost clouds in front of her face. "Now what?"

The question looped in her head a few times, but the voice that had compelled her to climb out her bedroom window had no answer. She was on her own.

Someone slammed into her from behind— hard.

"Hey," she shouted, tumbling forward. After righting herself on frozen legs, she spun around to curse at the rude asshole—but the assailant was gone. She was stuck looking around, mean-mugging people until they looked at her suspect.

A sudden gust of wind plunged the temperature lower and numbed her face. She pulled her coat collar up, but it didn't help.

The crowd ebbed and flowed, but she stood in one spot like she'd grown roots, still not knowing what to do. And after another twenty minutes, she felt stupid—and cold. Mostly cold.

Go back into the station—thaw out and think. However, when she looked at the large and imposing station, she couldn't get herself to put one foot in front of the other. She had the overwhelming sense that her returning inside would be a sign of defeat, because, once she was inside, it wouldn't be too hard to convince herself to get back on the train, go home and let *him* win . . . again.

Icy tears skipped down her face. *I can't go back.* Forcing her head down, she walked. She passed commuters yelling for cabs, huddled friends laughing—some singing, with no destination in mind. East of the station was bathed in complete darkness. She could barely make out anything in front of her. The only way she could deal with her growing fear was to ignore it. Ignore how its large, skeletal fingers wrapped around her throat. Ignore how it twisted her stomach into knots. Ignore how it scraped her spine raw.

Just keep walking.

"Help me," a feeble voice called out. "Help!"

Abrianna glanced around, not sure from which direction the voice had come. *Am I losing my mind now?*

"Help. I'm not drunk!"

It came from her right, in the middle of the road, where cars and taxis crept.

"I'm not drunk!" the voice yelled.

Finally, she made out a body lying next to a

concrete divider—the kind work crews used to block off construction areas.

"Help. Please!"

Again, Abrianna looked around the crowds of people streaming past. Didn't anyone else hear this guy? Even though that side of the building was dark, it was still heavily populated. Why was no one else responding to this guy's cry for help?

"Help. I'm not drunk!"

Timidly, she stepped off the sidewalk and skulked into the street. As vehicles headed toward her, she held up her hand to stop some and weaved in between others. Finally, Abrianna stood above a crumpled old man, in the middle of the road, and was at a loss as to what to do.

"I'm not drunk. I'm a diabetic. Can you help me up?" the man asked.

"Uh, sure." She knelt, despite fear, and asked, *What if it's a trap?*

It *could* be a trap, Abrianna reasoned even as she wrapped one of the guy's arms around her neck. Then, using all of her strength, she tried to help him to his feet, but couldn't. A Good Samaritan materialized out of nowhere to help her out.

"Whoa, man. Are you okay?" the stranger asked.

Abrianna caught glimpse of the Good Samaritan's shoulder-length stringy blond hair as a passing cab's headlights rolled by. He was ghost white with ugly pockmarks.

"Yes. Yes," the fallen guy assured. "It's my blood sugar. If you could just help me back over to the sidewalk that would be great."

"Sure. No problem," the blond stranger said.

Together, they helped the old black man back across the street.

"Thank you. I really appreciate this."

"No problem," the white guy said, his teeth briefly illuminated by another passing car as a smoker's yellow.

Once back on the sidewalk, he released the old man. "You two have a happy New Year!" As quick as the blond savior had appeared, he disappeared back into the moving crowd.

The old guy, huffing and puffing thick frost clouds, wrapped his hand around a NO PARKING sign and leaned against it.

"Are you sure you're all right?" Abrianna asked. It seemed wrong to leave him like this.

He nodded. "I'm a little dizzy, but it will pass. Thank you now."

That should be that. She had done what she could for the man. It was best that she was on her way. But she didn't move—probably because he didn't *look* okay.

As she suspected, he started sliding down the pole, his legs giving out. Abrianna wrapped his arm back around her neck to hold him up. "I got you," she said. But the question was: for how long?

"Thank you, child. Thank you."

Again, she didn't know what to do next. Maybe she should take him up to the station. At least, inside, she could get him to a bench or chair to sit down. "Can you walk?"

"Yes. I—I think so."

"No. No. Not back there," he said, refusing to move in the direction of the station. "They done already kicked me out tonight and threatened to lock me up if I return."

His words hit her strange. "What do you mean?"

He sighed. "Let's just go the other way."

With little choice, she did as he asked. It took a while, but the man's stench finally drifted under her nose. It was a strange, sour body odor that fucked with her gag reflexes. "Where do you want me to take you?" she asked, growing tired as he placed more and more of his weight on her shoulders.

When the old man didn't answer, she assumed he hadn't heard her. "Where are you trying to go?"

"Well . . . to be honest. Nowhere in particular," he said. "Just somewhere I can rest this old body and stay warm tonight. I read in one of the papers that it's supposed to dip down to nine degrees."

It hit her. "You don't have anywhere to sleep?"

"Well—of course I do. These here streets are my home. I got a big open sky as my roof, some good, hard concrete or soft grass as my floor. The rest usually takes care of itself." He chuckled—a mistake, judging by the way it set off the most godawful cough she'd ever heard.

They stopped when the coughing continued. Abrianna swore something rattled inside of his chest.

"Are you all right?" she asked. "Do you need a doctor?"

More coughing. *Are his lungs trying to come up?*

After what seemed like forever, he stopped, wheezed for air, and then wiped his face. "Sorry about that," he said, sounding embarrassed.

"It's okay," she said, resuming their walk.

"I really appreciate you for helping me out like this. I know I must be keeping you from wherever it is you're trying to get to. It's New Year's Eve and all."

"No. It's all right. I don't mind."

He twisted his head toward her and, despite the growing dark, she could make out his eyes scrutinizing her. "You're awfully *young* to be out here by yourself."

Abrianna ignored the comment and kept walking.

"How old are you?" he asked.

"Why?" she snapped, ready to drop him right there on the sidewalk and take off.

"Because you look like my grandbaby the last time I saw her. 'Bout sixteen, I'd say she was."

Abrianna jutted up her chin.

"She had a beautiful heart, too." He smiled. "Never could see any person or animal hurting."

The unexpected praise made her smile.

"Ah, yeah. A beautiful smile to boot."

They crossed the street to Second Avenue. She'd gotten used to his weight already, appreciated the extra body heat—but the *stench* still made her eyes water. *Did he say that it was going to get down to nine degrees tonight?* Abrianna had stolen cash from her house before she'd left, but hadn't had time to count all of it. Maybe she could get a hotel room—just for the night. After that, she would have to be careful about her finances. Once the money was gone—it was gone. She had no idea on how she and Shawn were going to get more.

Still walking, Abrianna pulled herself out of her troubled thoughts to realize that she and the old man had entered a park—a dark park— away from the streaming holiday crowd.

"Where are we going?" she asked, trying not to sound alarmed.

"Oh, just over there on that bench is fine." The old man pointed a shaky finger to their right. When they reached it, he dropped onto the iron bench like a sack of bricks and panted out more frosted air. "Whew," he exclaimed.

"That walk is getting harder and harder every day."

"You come here often?" Abrianna glanced around, catching a few figures, strolling. "Is it safe?"

"That depends," he said, patting the empty space next to him.

She took the hint and plopped down. "Depends on what?"

"On your definition of safe," he chuckled and set off another series of hard-to-listen-to coughs.

Abrianna wished that he'd stop trying to be a jokester. His lungs couldn't handle it. She watched him go through another painful episode.

At the end, he swore, "Goddamn it." Then he was contrite. "Oh. Sorry about that, sweetheart."

Smiling, she clued him in, "I've heard worse."

He nodded. "I reckon you have. Kids nowadays have heard and seen it all long *before* puberty hits. That's the problem: The world don't got no innocence anymore."

"Doesn't have any," she corrected him.

He chuckled. "Beauty and brains. You're a hell of a combination, kid."

Abrianna warmed toward the old man.

"Trouble at home?" he asked, his black gaze steady on her.

"No," she lied without really selling it. Why should she care if he believed her? In a few minutes, she'd probably never see him again.

"Nah. I didn't think so," he played along.

"You don't look like the type who would need-lessly worry her parents."

Abrianna sprung to her feet. "Looks like you're cool here. I gotta get going and find my friend."

"So the parents are off limits, huh?" He nod-ded. "Got it."

She stared at him, figuring out whether he was working an angle. Probably. Older people always did.

"It's tough out here, kid." His eyes turned sad before he added, "Dangerous too."

"I'm not looking for a speech."

"Fair enough." He pulled in a deep breath. "It's hypothermia season. Do you know what this is?"

"Yeah," Abrianna lied again.

"It means that folks can freeze to death out here—and often do. If you got somewhere safe to go, then I suggest you go there tonight. I'd hate to see someone as pretty as you wind up down at the morgue."

"I can take care of myself."

"Yeah? Have you ever done it before?"

"You sure do ask a lot of questions," she said.

"Believe it or not, you're not the first person to tell me that—bad habit, I suppose. But I've gotten too old to change now."

"What about you?" Abrianna challenged. "Aren't you afraid of freezing to death?"

He laughed, this time managing not to

choke over his lungs. "Oh, I *wish*—but the devil don't want nothing to do with me these days. I keep expecting to see him, but he never comes."

"You talk like you want to die."

"It's not about what I want, little girl. It's just time, that's all," he said quietly.

Abrianna didn't know what to say to that—but she did know that she could no longer feel her face. "Well, I gotta go."

He nodded. "I understand. You take care of yourself—and if you decide to stay out here—trust *no one.*"

She nodded and backpedaled away. It still felt wrong to leave the old guy there—especially if that whole freezing-to-death stuff was true. At that moment, it felt true.

The hotels were packed—or wanted nearly three hundred dollars for *one* night. That was more than half of Abrianna's money, she found out. At the last hotel, she agreed to the figure, but then they wanted to see some sort of ID. The front desk woman suggested she try a *motel* in another district—or a shelter.

An hour later, Abrianna was lost. Walking and crying through a row of creepy-looking houses, she had no idea where she was or where she was going.

Suddenly, gunshots were fired.

Abrianna ran and ducked down a dark alley.

Tires squealed.

Seconds later, a car roared past her.

More gunshots fired.

The back window of the fleeing muscle car exploded. The driver swerved and flew up onto a curb, and rammed headlong into a utility pole.

Bam!

The ground shook and the entire row of streetlights went out.

No way the driver survived that shit. Extending her neck around the corner of a house, Abrianna attempted to get a better look at what was going on, but at the sound of rushing feet pounding the concrete, she ducked back so that she could peep the scene. She counted seven guys running up to the car. When they reached the driver's side, a rumble of angry voices filled the night before they released another round of gunfire.

Holy shit. Abrianna backed away, spun around, and ran smack into a solid body.

The pockmarked Good Samaritan materialized out of the shadow. "Hey there, little girl. Remember me?"

Abrianna screamed. . . .

Mary B. Morrison's
If I Can't Have You series

If I Can't Have You
What really makes a man plunge headlong into obsession? And what does he do once he's past the point of no return? Find out in this seductive, mesmerizing tale of "love" gone dangerously wrong.

I'd Rather Be With You
With Madison's marriage on the rocks, Loretta couldn't resist looking after Chicago's interests and reigniting his passion for life. But now Madison wants to take back what's no longer hers . . .

If You Don't Know Me
The scandalous story of two women, a sizzling wager, and the fallout that's turned lives upside down. Now, with the only man they've ever wanted at stake, who will go one step too far to claim him?

Available wherever books and
ebooks are sold.